CONTENTS

KARATE COUNTDOWN

SPORT STORIES

illustrated by Sean Tiffany

text by Eric Stevens

raintree
a Capstone company — publishers for children

Raintree is an imprint of Capstone Global Library Limited, a company incorporated in England and Wales having its registered office at 264 Banbury Road, Oxford, OX2 7DY – Registered company number: 6695582

www.raintree.co.uk
myorders@raintree.co.uk

Designed by Carla Zetina-Yglesias
Original illustrations © Capstone Global Library Limited 2018
Illustrated by Sean Tiffany
Production by Tori Abraham
Originated by Capstone Global Library Limited
Printed and bound in China

ISBN 978 1 4747 3236 9
21 20 19 18 17
10 9 8 7 6 5 4 3 2 1

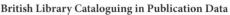

British Library Cataloguing in Publication Data
A full catalogue record for this book is available from the British Library.

CHAPTER 1

TROUBLE

Kenny Parks leaned against the passenger window of his dad's car. They were driving down Elm Street after a meeting with the headteacher at Kenny's school. The school year had just started, and Kenny was already in trouble.

"I'm pretty disappointed with you, Ken," his dad said. "I really thought that this year was going to be different from last year."

Ever since his mother died, Kenny seemed to get into trouble all the time. For some reason, Kenny would get angry very easily. He would talk back to teachers. Sometimes he even shouted at them.

"I just wish I understood why you can't get along with any of your teachers," his dad said as he turned onto their street.

Kenny shrugged. "It's not my fault, Dad," he said. "Teachers never like me!"

Kenny dropped his head. His mum had been a teacher, but that was a long time ago. "Look, Dad, I'm sorry," Kenny said.

Dad parked the car in front of their house. "I know you're sorry, Ken," he said. "You're always sorry, but nothing has changed. I think it's time to do something about this."

Kenny felt his face get hot. "What do you mean?" he asked.

"Well, when I was a boy, I used to get angry sometimes," Dad said. "So I started a karate class. It really helped."

Dad had often talked about his childhood karate lessons. He had really loved them, and he wanted Kenny to love karate too. But apart from playing basketball with his friends, Kenny had never been a big fan of sports. He wasn't interested in lessons of any kind.

Kenny rolled his eyes. "I don't want to take karate lessons, Dad," he said. He opened his car door.

Dad put his hand on Kenny's arm. "Sorry, Ken," Dad said. "It's already done. I've signed you up for a class. Your first lesson is this Saturday at eight."

"Eight in the morning?" Kenny replied, nearly shouting. "On a Saturday? That's not fair!"

Dad got out of the car and walked towards their house. His keys jingled in his hands.

"Maybe it's not fair," Dad said. "But we've got to do something about how you've been behaving."

Kenny followed him across the yard towards the front door of their house. "Dad!" he said.

"It's final, Ken," Dad replied. "You're learning karate." He opened the front door and walked inside.

Great, Kenny thought. *So much for my weekends.*

CHAPTER 2
ROBES

Most weeks, Kenny looked forward to the weekend. Usually, it felt like the weekend would never come. But that week, Kenny was not excited about the weekend. For some reason, the week flew by. Before Kenny knew it, his alarm clock was going off. It was 7:30 am on Saturday.

"Rise and shine, Ken!" his dad called from the kitchen. "I'm making sausage and eggs for breakfast."

Kenny took a deep breath through his nose. He could smell the sausages in the oven.

Well, Kenny thought, *at least I'll get an amazing breakfast.*

"We need to leave in 15 minutes," Dad said. "You can't be late for your first day at karate!"

"Okay," Kenny called. "I'm coming."

Kenny threw on some jeans and a sweatshirt. He sat down at the kitchen table and started wolfing down his breakfast.

"What are you wearing?" his dad asked, smirking.

Kenny stopped eating. He looked down at his sweatshirt and jeans. "What's wrong?" he said. "I always dress like this."

Dad shook his head. "Not this morning," he said. "Take a look in the gym bag on the chair next to you."

Kenny frowned. He reached over and grabbed the bag.

"What is it?" he asked.

"Open it," Dad replied.

Kenny opened the bag. He looked inside and pulled out a heavy white shirt and a pair of white trousers.

"Karate robes!" his dad said, smiling.

"Are you joking?" Kenny asked, eyes wide. "Do I have to wear this thing?"

Dad got up to refill his coffee. "Of course," he said. "What did you think you would wear for karate?"

"I'll look like an idiot!" Kenny said.

Dad sipped his coffee and sat down with the paper. "Nah," he said, "you'll look like everyone else in your class. Go and get changed."

"Come on!" Kenny yelled. "This is so stupid!"

Without looking up from his newspaper, Kenny's dad said, "Try saying thank you instead. These karate lessons and robes aren't free, you know."

Kenny started to walk back to his room. But his dad stood up. "Wait a second, Kenny," Dad said. "Don't forget your belt!"

Dad reached out and handed Kenny a white strip of cloth. "At first, you'll wear a white belt with your robes," Dad explained. "As you get better and better, you'll get a new belt as you reach each new level. It's pretty cool."

Kenny rolled his eyes as he grabbed the belt from his dad. He stomped back down the corridor to his room to change.

Could this day get any worse? he thought.

CHAPTER 3

SENSEI

The karate school was in a shopping centre. It was near the bus station.

"Is this it?" Kenny asked as his dad parked at the front. "This place looks awful."

"Don't judge a book by its cover," Dad replied. "I'll pick you up in an hour."

Kenny sighed as he climbed out of the car. He slammed the car door behind him and headed towards the karate school.

"Welcome," a small man said as Kenny walked in. "Please stand along the wall with the other students."

"Okay," Kenny replied. He looked to his right. About ten other boys were already there, dressed in robes and white belts just like him. They were standing against the wall, staring straight ahead.

The small man wore a black belt with his white robes. Kenny had heard enough about karate from his dad to know that a black belt meant the man was a karate master.

Kenny walked over to an empty spot near the middle of the group. "What is this, the army?" he joked to the boy next to him.

The boy smiled, but didn't look at him or reply. Kenny shrugged.

"Students," said the small man at the front of the room, "thank you for joining our karate class."

The man bowed. Kenny watched as the other students bowed back at him. Quickly, he followed their lead and bowed as well.

"We will begin today with how to tie your belt," the teacher said. "I can see that some of your belts are a little sloppy. Please remove them and I will show you the correct way to tie them."

The other students all undid their belts. Kenny chuckled. "Next he's going to show us how to tie our shoes!" he said to the boy next to him.

"If your shoes are as sloppy as your belt," the teacher said, "then, yes, I will help you with your shoes."

Kenny rolled his eyes. "My robe is closed," Kenny replied. "It looks like my belt is doing its job."

"The belt does not only close the robe," the teacher answered. "It shows others what kind of student you are."

"Then I suppose I'm a sloppy student, sir," Kenny said. His voice was tense and angry.

"Sensei," the teacher replied sternly. "In karate, we use the Japanese word *sensei*, not *sir*."

Kenny felt his face getting hot. He pulled off his belt.

"And we reply, 'Yes, Sensei,'" the man added.

Kenny looked down at the floor. "Yes, Sensei," he said quietly.

CHAPTER 4

MONDAY

Monday morning was almost a relief to Kenny. He had been sore from his karate class for the entire weekend. After learning how to tie their belts, the class had done some jumping jacks and sit-ups to warm up. Then Sensei had showed them how to punch.

Kenny slouched in his chair before his first class at school on Monday morning. He rubbed his shoulder.

"What's wrong with you?" Craig Peters asked from the desk next to Kenny.

"My whole body is sore," Kenny replied.

"Did you get into a fight again this weekend?" Craig asked.

"No, I didn't get in a fight," Kenny snapped. "Why, do you want to start something?"

Craig laughed and threw up his hands. "Calm down!" he said.

Craig had known Kenny for years, and he knew Kenny wouldn't start a real fight with him. They were friends. But he had seen Kenny in a few bad fights over the years with other children.

Kenny scowled. "My dad signed me up for karate lessons," he said.

"Nice!" Craig replied. He sliced the air with one hand, then the other. "Hiya!" he said.

Kenny rolled his eyes.

"You'll be a ninja in no time," Craig added.

"It's not like that at all, believe me," Kenny said.

"It's not?" Craig asked. "No wicked chops and flying kicks and fighting ten ninjas at once?"

Kenny just shook his head. "Not at all," he said. "It's more like making the students feel like idiots and showing them how to tie their shoes."

The bell rang. "Okay, class," Ms Riaz announced. "Let's get started."

"Tie their shoes?" Craig whispered, leaning over.

Kenny nodded. "Pretty much," he said. "It's really stupid."

CHAPTER 5
CONTROL

That week went by quickly. It wasn't a terrible week. There were no meetings with the headteacher, but Kenny did talk back a few times to Ms Riaz.

At his karate lesson on Saturday, Kenny lined up with the other students. He made sure his belt was tied correctly.

Sensei bowed. Kenny bowed back with the other students.

"Today," Sensei said, "we will work on blocking. You will be able to defend yourselves against the punches we learned last week."

Sensei stepped to the middle of the mat. "I will show you several blocks before we begin," he said. "Mr Parks, you will attack."

Kenny opened his eyes wide. "Me?" he asked, shocked.

"Me, Sensei," the teacher corrected. "And yes, you, Mr Parks. Please stand here in your punching stance."

Kenny stepped forward and stood on the mat. He faced Sensei. Then he spread his feet and bent his elbows. He was in the punching stance he had learned the week before.

"Good stance, Mr Parks," the teacher said. "Attack me whenever you feel like you are ready."

"You want me to punch you, Sensei?" Kenny asked, surprised.

"I want you to try to punch me," Sensei replied, smiling.

Kenny inhaled deeply and clenched his fists. He thought back to the last week of class and remembered the way to do a punch to the chest.

He took a step forward. With a loud grunt, he punched.

As fast as lightning, Sensei blocked the punch with his left arm. Then, before Kenny could pull his arm back, Sensei lifted him by the elbow and dropped him onto his back.

In less than a second, Sensei was standing over Kenny. Kenny stared up at him from the mat.

"Ow," Kenny moaned.

Sensei turned to the class. "Do you see, students," he said, "how I used Mr Parks' energy against him?"

"Yes, Sensei!" the others replied.

Kenny was angry. Sensei had made him look like a fool!

Kenny jumped to his feet and ran at his teacher. "Block this!" he shouted. He charged at the small man.

"Gladly," Sensei replied. He calmly stepped aside and gently caught Kenny by the shoulder. In less than a second, Kenny was on his back again.

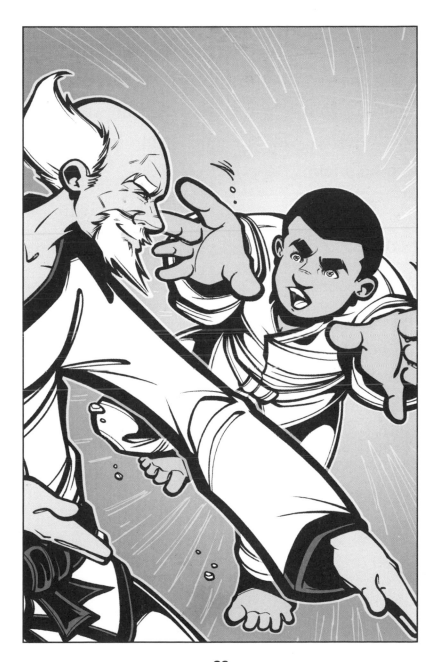

Sensei kneeled over Kenny. "Mr Parks," the teacher said quietly. "You must learn to control your anger. Otherwise, your anger will control you." He reached out his hand to help Kenny up.

Kenny got to his feet with Sensei's help. "That's easy for you to say," Kenny said under his breath.

* * *

An hour later, the class had finished. Sensei had been Kenny's partner for all the sparring. Somehow, Kenny had managed to stay on his feet most of the time, except whenever he'd become angry.

The class lined up. "Very well done today, students," Sensei said. "I will let you go in a moment. First, I have an announcement."

Kenny glanced at the other students. All of them kept their eyes straight ahead.

"In three weeks," Sensei continued, "we will have a class tournament. Every year, we hold a tournament for the students in each level's class."

He smiled. "Being in the tournament is required," Sensei added. "The winner of the tournament will earn the respect of his Sensei and his classmates. He will also receive free lessons for the next level of training."

Some of the students smiled or cheered. "Cool," said the boy next to Kenny.

"Thank you, students," Sensei finished. He bowed. All of the students, including Kenny, bowed back. Then they went outside to wait for their lifts home.

"I really want to win that tournament," one of the boys told Kenny as they waited.

Kenny shrugged. "I doubt I have a chance," he said. "Did you see the way Sensei threw me around in there?"

The other boy laughed. "That just means you get more practice than the rest of us," he said. "And sparring against Sensei is better practice than sparring against one of us."

Kenny nodded. "That's true," he replied.

The other boy kept talking, but Kenny wasn't paying attention to him.

Hmm, Kenny thought. *Maybe I do have a shot at winning the tournament.*

CHAPTER 6

MELTDOWN

"Another rough karate lesson?" Craig asked before their first lesson on Monday.

Kenny groaned. "Afraid so," he replied.

"What happened?" his friend asked. "Did the teacher pick on you again?"

Kenny nodded. "Even worse than last time," he replied. He rolled up the sleeve of his T-shirt. There was a big purple bruise.

"Whoa!" Craig said. "That's a nice one. How'd you get that?"

Kenny shook his head. "Craig, you wouldn't believe me," he said.

"Try me," Craig said.

Kenny looked around the classroom before answering to make sure no one was listening. "I attacked him on Saturday," he whispered.

"The teacher? You attacked your teacher?" Craig asked, stunned.

Kenny nodded slowly, smiling a little. "Can you believe it?" he asked.

"To be honest, yes!" Craig replied. "I think you'd attack Jackie Chan if he made you angry."

Ms Riaz walked in. Then the bell rang.

"Don't start with me, Craig!" Kenny said quietly. Craig chuckled and opened his notebook.

"Good morning, everyone," Ms Riaz said. "Can I have three volunteers to write the answers to the homework on the board, please?"

Kenny looked around. As usual, no one volunteered.

After a moment, Ms Riaz sighed. "Okay then, I'll choose three people," she said.

Everyone, including Kenny, slouched a little in their seats. No one wanted to be chosen.

"Okay, question number one, Hanna," Ms Riaz said. Hanna stood up.

"Number two, Jay, please," Ms Riaz went on.

"Yes," Craig said in a whisper.

"One more," Kenny said, crossing his fingers.

Ms Riaz looked at him. She said "Kenny, come on up and do number three, please."

Craig pointed at Kenny. "You're the man," Craig said, laughing.

Kenny pulled his homework out of his notebook. He walked up to the white board.

Ms Riaz handed him a marker. "Thank you, Kenny," she said.

Kenny glanced at the work the other two students were doing. They were going through their maths problems quickly.

He looked down at his homework. His handwriting was sloppy, and he was sure his answer for question number three was wrong.

Slowly, he raised the marker. He started copying the problem onto the board.

Maths, Kenny thought. *What a waste of time! Like I'll ever need to know this stuff in real life.*

He finished writing his answer on the board. Then he stood back and looked at it. He had no idea if his answer was right.

With a shrug, Kenny threw the marker back on the tray. Then he went back to his desk.

"I don't think your answer's right," Craig whispered as Kenny sat down. "I got 42."

Kenny looked up at his answer. He had written 117. If Craig was right, Kenny wasn't even close.

Great, Kenny thought.

He barely paid attention as the class went over the first two problems. Then it was time for number three.

"Okay, Kenny," Ms Riaz said. "For question three, you came up with 117."

Kenny shrugged. "I suppose," he said.

"Can you explain how you came up with that answer?" Ms Riaz asked.

"No," Kenny mumbled.

"You can't explain?" Ms Riaz asked, frowning.

"What's the point?" Kenny snapped. He knocked his textbook off his desk. It hit the ground with a thud. "I got it wrong, didn't I?"

Ms Riaz sighed. "Okay, Kenny," she said. "I'll talk to you after class."

* * *

When the bell rang to end the class, everyone hurried to leave. Craig whispered, "Good luck, Jackie Chan," before he left the classroom.

Ms Riaz walked over to Kenny's desk. She said, "Kenny, this isn't the first time we've had this conversation, is it?"

Kenny shrugged. "I suppose not," he said.

"I can see that these maths problems are frustrating you," Ms Riaz went on. "However, if you let your frustration take over, you'll never find the right answer."

"I know," Kenny said. He thought about all the time he spent on the mat when he sparred with Sensei.

"Do I need to set up another meeting with the headteacher and your father?" Ms Riaz asked.

Kenny sighed. "No," he said. "You don't need to call my dad."

"You know, sometimes I get frustrated with a maths problem," Ms Riaz began.

"You get frustrated with maths problems?" Kenny asked, shocked.

"Of course!" Ms Riaz said. "Everyone does sometimes."

Kenny sat back in his chair. "Oh," he muttered. He wondered if Sensei ever got angry.

CHAPTER 7

BENCHED

"Today, students, we will begin with sparring," Sensei said. The students were lined up against the wall to begin their class.

"Mr Parks," Sensei added, "I will let you practise with someone else today. Everyone, please choose a partner."

Everyone picked a partner. Kenny ended up with a boy called Steve Shaw. A couple of students spread their feet and got ready to do some punches.

"Students!" Sensei interrupted. "Don't forget to bow."

All the students brought their feet together. They stood up straight.

First, everyone turned to bow at Sensei. Then they turned and bowed at their partners.

"Thank you," Sensei said, smiling. "Begin!"

At first, it was pretty messy. Kenny got into position and pulled back a fist to punch. At the same time, Steve started to punch.

"This isn't working," Kenny said, laughing. "I'll block first."

Steve nodded. "Cool," he said. "You had all that practice punching Sensei last week anyway!"

Steve drew his elbow in and tightened his fists. Kenny was ready to block.

Steve counted off with a sharp shout. Then he moved forward and started to attack Kenny.

Kenny blocked quickly. He stopped several punches by snapping his arm across his stomach.

"Hi-YA!" he cried as he brushed Steve's punches aside. "Hi-YA!"

"Very good, Mr Parks!" Sensei called out as he walked past them. "Try to stay focused, Mr Shaw!" he added to Kenny's partner.

Then Kenny accidentally blocked to the right when he should have blocked to the left. One of Steve's punches got through and struck him hard in the chest.

Before he knew what had happened, Kenny was on the mat. For a moment, he felt like he couldn't breathe.

Steve leaned over him. "Are you okay?" he asked. He put out his hand to help Kenny up.

Kenny didn't take it. Instead, he slapped Steve's hand away.

"I'm fine!" Kenny snapped.

"Are you?" Sensei asked, walking over. He stood next to Steve. "You sound angry," Sensei went on. "You're letting your feelings control you."

"So what?" Kenny said. He got to his feet. Then he turned to face Steve. "It's my turn to attack," Kenny said.

"No," Sensei said. "It's your turn to sit down."

"What?" Kenny said. "That's not fair!"

"Fair?" Sensei said. "Who said anything about fair? You will sit on the bench and look at the street through the window."

Kenny clenched his fists. He felt his face getting hot.

"A bus stops in front of this school every ten minutes," Sensei added. "You will watch the bus stop and count how many people get off."

"Are you joking?" Kenny asked.

Sensei turned away. "Class, continue sparring, please!" he said. "The first round of the tournament is coming soon!"

Kenny was cross. He sat down on the bench and faced the window. Soon, the bus pulled up.

Well, this is boring, Kenny thought. He watched the people get off. First was an old lady. She took forever to walk down the steps.

"One," Kenny muttered.

Three high school girls stepped off after the old lady. "Two, three and four," Kenny said.

Then the bus doors closed. It drove off.

"Four, Sensei!" Kenny called out. He turned to face the classroom again.

"Face the window, Mr Parks," Sensei replied. "Don't call out the numbers. You will tell me later."

Kenny rolled his eyes and turned back to the window. There wasn't much to look at outside. It was just a boring street in his boring city.

Across the street was a car dealership. Next to that was a restaurant, and next to that was a grocery store. None of them were even open yet this early on a Saturday.

Kenny could hear the other students sparring behind him. "Hi-YA!" they cried out as they sparred.

Kenny started to get angry. He hated listening to them spar while he just sat there. Just then, the bus pulled up again. The door hissed when it opened.

A big man stepped carefully off the bus. He was carrying a paper bag. "One," Kenny muttered to himself.

A young mother followed. She was pulling her daughter behind her. The little girl was crying.

"Two, three," Kenny said. He took a deep breath.

After the mother and child, two kids about Kenny's age hopped off the bus. They were laughing and joking around.

"Four and five," Kenny said. He took another deep breath.

Finally, a middle-aged woman stepped out, talking on her mobile phone. Then the doors closed.

"Six," Kenny said. "Plus the four from before . . . that makes ten."

The morning went on like that. Kenny watched the bus stop and counted the people getting off.

By the time the class was over, he didn't even notice the students behind him, even with all the shouting.

After dismissing the rest of the class, Sensei went over to Kenny. "So, Mr Parks," Sensei said. "What did you learn today?"

"Well," Kenny said, "I counted forty-two people in total."

Sensei smiled. "The number does not matter," he said.

"It doesn't?" Kenny asked. "Then why did I have to count everyone?"

"It's not the answer you needed," Sensei replied. "It's the counting itself."

"I don't get it," Kenny said.

"Did you feel calmer as you counted?" Sensei asked.

"Yes," Kenny admitted.

"Then that's what you needed," Sensei said.

CHAPTER 8

COUNTING

"Did you give up karate?" Craig asked the next Monday in their maths class. "You don't look hurt today."

"The last class was odd," Kenny said. But just then, Ms Riaz walked in and the bell rang.

"Good morning, everyone," Ms Riaz said. "Let's take a look at the homework. Any volunteers to show your work on the white board?"

Kenny looked around the room. As usual, no one volunteered.

"She's going to call on me," Kenny whispered to Craig. "I know it."

"After what happened last week?" Craig said. "No way!"

Kenny nodded. "You'll see," he said.

He was right. For the third problem, Ms Riaz called on Kenny.

Kenny pulled his homework out of his notebook and went up to the board. Ms Riaz handed him a marker. "Thanks," Kenny said, without thinking about it.

Ms Riaz looked shocked. "Thank you, Kenny," she replied.

Kenny looked down at his homework. It was a mess, as usual. He started to get frustrated.

I just can't do this stuff, he thought. He was sure the answer on his paper was wrong again.

Kenny wrote the problem on the board. Then he stood back and looked at it.

I can't do this! he thought again. The numbers in front of him started to blur. He couldn't even see straight. He was getting angry.

Then Kenny thought about his last karate class. "It's not the answer you needed, Mr Parks," Sensei had said. "It is the counting itself." Kenny remembered feeling calmer as he counted.

Kenny closed his eyes and thought about the bus stop. He thought about the people he had counted. He pictured them in his head.

Number 1, the slow old lady. Numbers 2, 3 and 4, the high school girls. Number 5, the man with his groceries. Numbers 6 and 7, the mother and her little girl.

As he counted and breathed slowly, Kenny felt himself relaxing. He looked back at the board. The numbers weren't blurry anymore. The question made sense.

Kenny smiled. He lifted the marker and started to write.

* * *

At the end of the lesson, Ms Riaz asked Kenny to talk to her.

"You did a good job today, Kenny," she said.

"Thanks," Kenny replied. "I can't believe I got that problem right."

"I can," Ms Riaz said. "I told you that if you could stop letting yourself get frustrated, you'd do well! I'm proud of you."

"Thanks," Kenny said.

Ms Riaz cleared her throat. "I hope you don't mind me saying this," she added. "Your mother and I were good friends when she taught here. She would be really proud of you."

Kenny swallowed hard and nodded. "I know," he said quietly.

CHAPTER 9

THE BIG DAY

The next few weeks flew by. Whenever Kenny got angry, he would think about the people getting off the bus. He counted them in his head. Every time, his anger faded.

Finally, the day of the tournament had arrived. The morning of the tournament, Kenny's dad drove him to the karate school.

"This is the big day, huh?" Dad asked.

Kenny shrugged, trying to hide his excitement. "Yeah, I guess," he said.

"Good luck," Dad said. "Don't break a leg, okay?"

Kenny laughed as he got out of the car. "I won't," he said.

In class, the students lined up against the wall. "Welcome, students," Sensei said. He smiled.

"As you know, today is the tournament," Sensei went on. "You will all pair up and spar. Each time you strike your opponent, you will earn a point. The winner, after earning three points, will move on in the tournament."

All the students seemed pretty excited. Some were even bouncing on their toes, ready to start.

"In an hour, we will have our class winner," Sensei said. "Count off!"

He paired the students into groups. Then they lined up and faced each other.

"Bow!" Sensei ordered. The class bowed at Sensei, then at each other.

"Begin!" Sensei said.

Kenny took a deep breath. Then he began.

It wasn't like normal sparring. No one spoke or asked who would attack first. They circled each other, looking for ways to strike.

The first four rounds went by quickly. Kenny had practised so many times with Sensei that the other students couldn't get past his blocks.

Before Kenny knew it, he had made it to the final round. It was between him and Steve Shaw.

They eyed each other and slowly circled. Steve moved forward.

"Hi-YA!" Steve shouted as he thrust his fist out. Kenny blocked it with ease.

Steve dropped to his knee and swept Kenny's foot. He caught Kenny's ankle and knocked him down.

"One!" Sensei called.

That was a point for Steve. Kenny knew he had to step it up, but he could feel himself starting to get angry.

They started to circle again. Kenny took a deep breath.

He stared into Steve's eyes. "One," Kenny said. "Old lady."

Steve squinted at him. "What?" he asked.

Kenny drew back his elbow. "Two," he said. "High school girl."

He stepped his right foot out and thrust his fist at Steve. "Hi-YA!" Kenny cried.

Steve blocked the punch. "Kenny, what are you talking about?" Steve asked.

Kenny took a deep breath. "Three," he muttered. "Four."

Steve stepped back, then snapped out his leg in a straight kick. "Yah!" he shouted.

Kenny dropped his arms and blocked the kick. "Five," he said. "Big man with groceries."

He pulled on Steve's ankles and dropped his opponent to the mat. "Hi-YA!" Kenny cried. He dropped his fist onto Steve's chest.

"One!" Sensei called out.

We're tied, Kenny thought.

They began to circle each other again. "Six," Kenny whispered. He took another deep breath.

Steve eyed him and then lunged forward. Kenny brushed the punch aside. Then he landed a kick on Steve's side.

"Two points!" Sensei called out.

Kenny smiled a little. He was winning two points to one.

Steve began to circle him. Kenny could tell Steve was getting frustrated now.

"Hi-YA!" Steve cried. He quickly threw three punches as he moved towards Kenny. Kenny blocked two of them, but one punch grazed his shoulder.

"Two points!" Sensei called out.

Kenny started to get angry. "What?" he said. Then he stopped himself.

He took a deep breath. "Seven," he said, closing his eyes. "Boy messing about."

He smiled again and faced Steve. Then he opened his eyes and exhaled slowly.

"Eight," Kenny said, moving forward. "Young mother."

He dropped to his knee and swept Steve's legs. Steve dropped to the mat with a thud.

Kenny quickly stood over him. He drew back his arm. "Nine!" Kenny cried out as he dropped his fist. "Little daughter!"

"Three points!" Sensei called out, stepping onto the mat. "Winner, Mr Parks!"

Kenny couldn't believe it. Smiling, he got to his feet and offered his hand to Steve.

"Nice match," Kenny said, helping Steve to his feet.

Steve nodded. "You too," he said. "But what was with all that counting?"

Kenny laughed. "It's a long story," he said. "Let's just say all my practice with Sensei paid off."

Kenny looked across the room and smiled at Sensei. Sensei smiled back. Then they both bowed.

ABOUT THE AUTHOR

Eric Stevens lives in Minnesota, USA. He is studying to become a middle-school English teacher. Some of his favourite things include pizza, playing video games, watching cooking shows on TV, riding his bike and trying new restaurants. Some of his least favourite things include olives and shovelling snow.

ABOUT THE ILLUSTRATOR

When Sean Tiffany was growing up, he lived on a small island off the coast of Maine, USA. Every day, from sixth grade until he graduated from high school, he had to take a boat to get to school. When Sean isn't working on his art, he works on a multimedia project called "OilCan Drive", which combines music and art. He has a pet cactus called Jim.

GLOSSARY

announcement something that is said publicly or officially

energy strength

focused if you are focused, you are concentrating on something

frustrated feeling helpless or discouraged

level position or rank

master expert

ninja person who is highly trained in ancient Japanese martial arts

opponent someone who is against you in a fight

required if you are required to do something, you must do it

respect feeling of admiration

tense nervous or worried

tournament series of contests in which a number of people try to win a championship

KARATE WORDS
YOU SHOULD KNOW

dojo practice area of a karate school

gi white robes worn in karate

karateka karate student

kata pattern of moves used by karate students to practise their skills

kyu rank, or belt colour

sensei teacher of a karate school

spar to practise the skills learned in karate classes. Blocks, kicks and punches are used with little physical contact.

stance body's position. There are several stances. Each stance is used for a type of attack or defence.

MORE ABOUT KARATE

Karate is a martial art, or a fighting style. Karate began in Japan. It was first taught in the United States in 1955, and first introduced to the UK in 1956.

Karate has ranks for levels of skill levels. Each rank has a different belt colour. White belts are for beginners. Black belts are for karate masters. It takes years of practice to earn a black belt in karate.

In karate, students learn self-defence. Students are taught many skills, including blocks, stances, punches and kicks. Students practise by sparring with each other.

Karate involves fighting, but it focuses on self-discipline. Students are taught to respect others and to use fighting as a last resort.

DISCUSSION QUESTIONS

1. Why does Sensei tell Kenny to count the people getting off the bus? How does the counting help Kenny?

2. When Kenny says that the karate school looks awful, Kenny's dad says, "Don't judge a book by its cover." Can you give other examples of things that shouldn't be judged by how they look?

3. Kenny uses the counting trick that Sensei taught him to stop feeling frustrated. Discuss other ways he could have overcome his frustration.

WRITING PROMPTS

1. Kenny's dad took karate lessons because he, too, had trouble controlling his anger. Pick a person in your family and write about how you are like that person.

2. When he's counting people getting off the bus (on pages 47 – 49), Kenny sees lots of different people. Choose one of the people he sees. Write a story about what that person might be doing that day. Don't forget to give the person a name!

3. Kenny wins the karate tournament. What do you think happens next? Write about it.

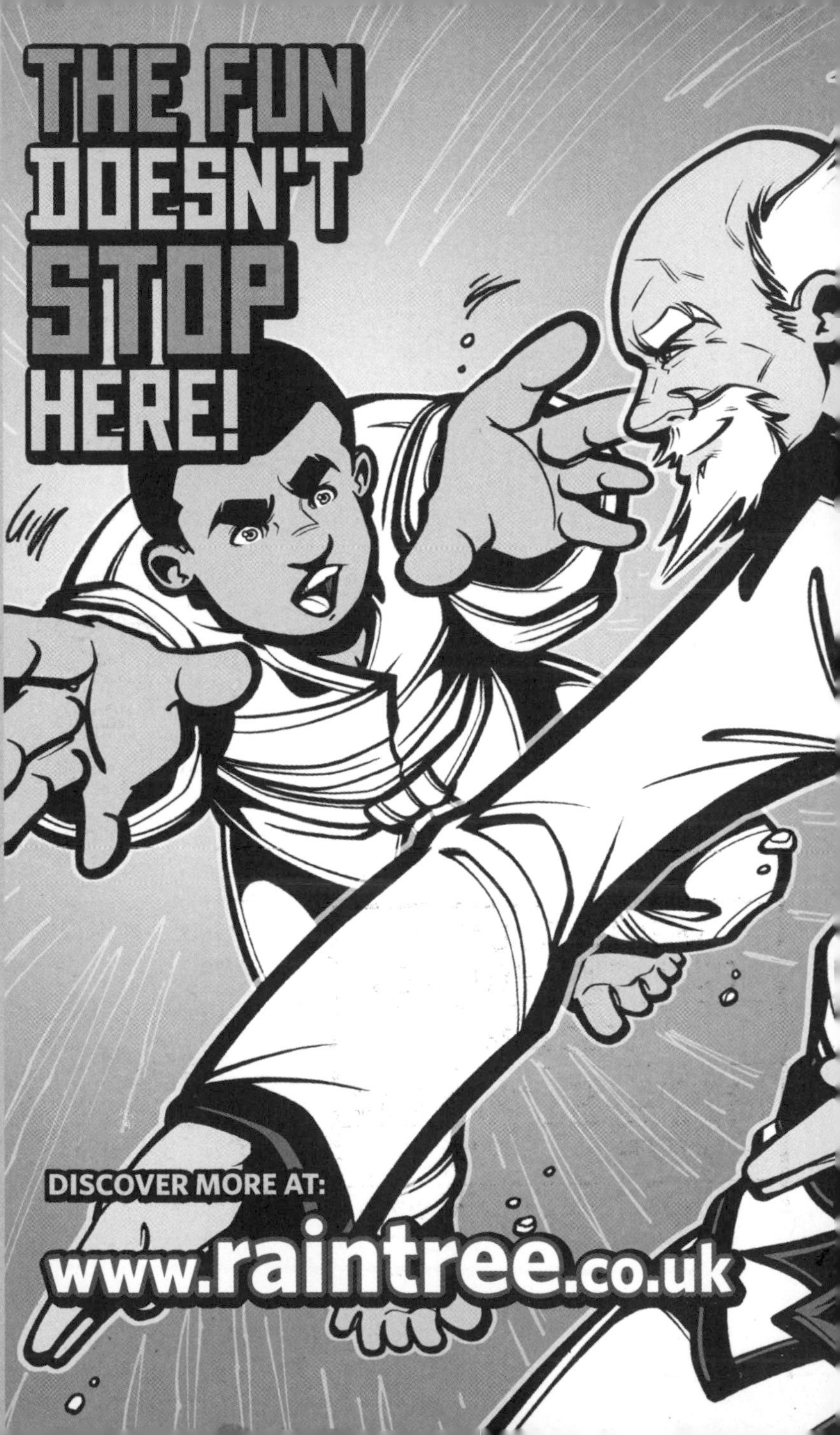
THE FUN DOESN'T STOP HERE!
DISCOVER MORE AT:
www.raintree.co.uk

Commentary

Act 1 Scene 1

Measure for Measure opens with mysteries that are never fully resolved during the course of the play: the Duke of Vienna is leaving the city; he gives no reason for his departure, nor does he explain why he is leaving Angelo to govern in his place. Although the Duke goes to some lengths to explain to Escalus that he would be the most experienced, knowledgeable and worthy substitute, he says he is not to be left in charge but is to be given a different 'commission' and is warned not to deviate from his instructions. The precise nature of the commission given to Escalus is not revealed to the audience.

The Duke asks Escalus for his opinion of Angelo's potential as 'substitute': 'What figure of us think you he will bear?' Describing the absolute power to be left with Angelo, the Duke says that he has 'Lent him our terror, dressed him with our love'. This is the first of a series of antitheses concerning the power given to Angelo. There are implications in the imagery: the power has only been 'lent', and Angelo is merely 'dressed' in the authority of the Duke, carrying the suggestion of a temporary abdication of power. There is a balance between 'terror' and 'love' in the power offered to Angelo, and the play explores the ways in which Angelo deals with these two extremes. Escalus agrees at this moment that there is no one more fitted to be the Duke's deputy.

When Angelo arrives, the Duke praises him and says that his outward behaviour demonstrates his personality to all those who see him. In a complex sentence, the Duke warns him not to keep his good qualities to himself:

> Thyself and thy belongings
> Are not thine own so proper as to waste
> Thyself upon thy virtues, they on thee.   *(lines 29–31)*

The Duke compares Nature to an investor, saying that she lends people talents and expects both gratitude and an increase on her investment, but then says that he is speaking to someone (Angelo) who is able to demonstrate this by his own example. In a metrically short line, 'Hold therefore, Angelo', perhaps indicating a change in tone, or a gesture, the Duke then tells Angelo that he is to be regent in Vienna. For the second time the Duke refers to the two extremes of a ruler's power: 'Mortality and mercy'. He is giving Angelo the power of life and death over the people of Vienna. Angelo is told that Escalus 'Though first in question, is [his] secondary'. Angelo hesitates before accepting his new role and, using an image taken from coining, asks for more trials to be made of his character before he takes up so great an honour.

> Let there be some more test made of my metal
> Before so noble and so great a figure
> Be stamped upon it. *(lines 48–50)*

The Duke refuses and insists that Angelo accept his 'honours'. He says that his departure is so urgent that he is leaving 'unquestioned / Matters of needful value', though he does not explain what they are. Angelo is anxious for more discussion, but the Duke will not even permit his two ministers to escort him part of the way. He reminds Angelo that he has absolute power:

> So to enforce or qualify the laws
> As to your soul seems good. *(lines 65–6)*

The Duke wants to leave secretly without formalities. He says that though he loves the people, he does not like to appear publicly before them, and that he does not consider anyone trustworthy who courts public opinion. (Shakespeare's Jacobean audience may well have identified these feelings as resembling those of King James, see page 65.) The Duke says that he will write, and he expects Angelo and Escalus to send him news. When the Duke has left, the two men leave together to talk over the exact nature of the commissions given to them.

Act 1 Scene 2

The tone changes as Lucio and two other Gentlemen talk over the prospects of war with Hungary. They speculate whether the Duke will form an alliance with other dukes. The Gentlemen pray for peace for their souls, but not peace on earth, as they look forward to fighting the Hungarian forces. Lucio accuses them of being like a pirate who

Shakespeare

Measure for Measure

Sheila Innes

Series Editor: Rex Gibson

CAMBRIDGE
UNIVERSITY PRESS

PUBLISHED BY THE PRESS SYNDICATE OF THE UNIVERSITY OF CAMBRIDGE
The Pitt Building, Trumpington Street, Cambridge, United Kingdom

CAMBRIDGE UNIVERSITY PRESS
The Edinburgh Building, Cambridge CB2 2RU, UK
40 West 20th Street, New York, NY 10011–4211, USA
477 Williamstown Road, Port Melbourne, VIC 3207, Australia
Ruiz de Alarcón 13, 28014 Madrid, Spain
Dock House, The Waterfront, Cape Town 8001, South Africa

http://www.cambridge.org

First published 2004

Printed in the United Kingdom at the University Press, Cambridge

Typeface 9.5/12pt Scala   *System* QuarkXPress®

A catalogue record for this book is available from the British Library

ISBN 0 521 53850 5 paperback

Cover image: © Getty Images/PhotoDisc

Contents

Introduction

'With what measure ye mete, it shall be measured to you again' (Matthew 7.2). There are few plays by Shakespeare where the title of the play is so insistently its theme. In every scene of the play one thing is measured or balanced by another. In *Measure for Measure* Shakespeare seems to be experimenting with a new style of play: one based on a debate concerning justice and mercy and what constitutes proper government of the self and the state. He asks his audience to make judgements as profound as those made by characters in the play.

The action of *Measure for Measure* takes place over five days – or several months – as there is double time-scheme in the play. The shorter time-scheme follows the fortunes of Claudio, who is condemned to die for getting pregnant the girl he has promised to marry; the longer time-scheme covers the absence of the Duke and the installation of Angelo as his deputy. Shakespeare had used a double time-scheme in other plays with great success, and in *Measure for Measure* it is particularly effective, as much of the emotional intensity of the play comes from the abruptness with which Angelo sentences Claudio, and the brevity of time available to Isabella.

Three major characters with an almost pathological denial of their sexuality are presented: Angelo, who 'scarce confesses / That his blood flows'; Isabella, who considers fornication as the worst possible sin, 'There is a vice that most I do abhor'; and the Duke who thinks that he is too mature to feel desire, 'Believe not that the dribbling dart of love / Can pierce a complete bosom'. The play requires each of them to reach a deeper understanding of themselves and of their emotions.

The play begins with unanswered questions. Why is the Duke leaving? Why should Angelo rather than Escalus be left as deputy? Why is Angelo to be tested? At its end, the play implicitly asks questions that are even more challenging. Is Angelo content with Mariana? Has he learned to temper justice with mercy? Why does Isabella say nothing to Claudio? How does Isabella react to the Duke's proposal? In performance, most of these questions must be tackled and some kind of answer given. The rich ambiguity of the play requires every reader to provide their own interpretations.

erased the biblical commandment against stealing. The Gentlemen and Lucio joke and taunt one another about their morals and sexually transmitted diseases. When Lucio accuses one Gentleman of being a 'wicked villain', he retorts that he and Lucio are as bad as one another, cut from the same length of cloth: 'there went but a pair of shears between us'. He then puns on 'piled' and 'French velvet', words which had obscene connotations.

When Mistress Overdone enters, Lucio and the Gentlemen continue to joke about the sexually transmitted diseases they have acquired by visiting her brothel. She tells them of the arrest of Claudio for getting a girl, called Juliet, pregnant. She says that he is 'worth five thousand of you all' and that he is to be executed for this offence within three days. The stress on the speed of the action concerning Claudio's execution is characteristic of the play. Lucio and the Gentlemen believe her story, partly because Claudio was supposed to have met Lucio and has not arrived, and partly because there has recently been a 'proclamation' concerning the enforcement of the law against fornication.

The men leave to find out more, and Mistress Overdone, briefly alone on stage, bewails all the reasons for the diminishing trade in prostitution: the soldiers are away fighting a war, sexually transmitted diseases are rife, her customers are being executed, and men are too poor to afford a prostitute. Pompey, her assistant, enters and reports that he has just seen a man being led to prison for getting a woman pregnant: 'Groping for trouts in a peculiar river.' As Mistress Overdone has already spoken of the arrest of Claudio, when she questions Pompey it is not made clear whether she thinks that this is another case of a man being arrested, or whether Shakespeare wanted to emphasise to the audience that Angelo had put punitive laws into action very swiftly. Pompey speaks in more detail of the proclamation mentioned by Lucio and the Gentlemen, telling her that all the brothels in the suburbs are to be destroyed (as Vienna in the play represents London, this would suggest those brothels on the south bank of the Thames – see page 69). Those in the city are to be allowed to remain, Pompey says, to 'seed' new ones. He says that 'a wise burgher put in for them', implying that someone with power and influence has found a way to evade the law. He comforts Mistress Overdone, saying cynically that a good brothel-keeper will never be short of customers.

Shakespeare ensures that the audience knows who enters next on stage by having Pompey identify Claudio, the Provost and Juliet. Claudio is shamed by being publicly shown to the world by the Provost, who is obeying Angelo's orders. Claudio recognises that 'Authority' has an arbitrary, but just power approaching that of the gods. Lucio joins him, and Claudio tells him that his imprisonment is the result of 'too much liberty' and that excesses are always followed by 'restraint' (punning on the official 'restraint' or arrest of his present situation). He uses the illustration of taking arsenical rat poison: once taken it causes a desperate thirst, but the satisfaction of that thirst will kill the drinker. Claudio takes his imprisonment seriously and does not attempt to defend himself. Lucio lightens the tone by commenting sardonically on Claudio's elaborate wordplay, and he asks what crime Claudio has committed. Claudio is at first reluctant to confess to 'lechery', but eventually explains that he and Juliet have privately, though not officially, married. Conventions concerning marriage were different in Shakespeare's time (see pages 67–9). They were waiting to make their marriage public until they had the agreement of Juliet's guardians, who have control of her dowry. He admits that they have slept together ('our most mutual entertainment') and that Juliet's resultant pregnancy has made their sexual congress public knowledge.

Explaining to Lucio that Angelo has revived a law against fornication that has been dormant for 19 years, Claudio speculates on the possible reasons for Angelo's severity. He wonders whether he is being made an example because Angelo intends to impress his new authority upon the general public, or whether the power given to him by the Duke has made Angelo into a tyrant, or even whether it is in Angelo's nature to be tyrannical. He finally decides that Angelo is enforcing this old law in order to enhance his reputation, his 'name'.

Lucio agrees, and cannot resist making a joke about Claudio's predicament. He suggests that Claudio should appeal to the absent Duke, but Claudio has already tried to and cannot find out where he is. Claudio would like his sister to make a final appeal to Angelo and he asks Lucio to be his messenger, telling him that Isabella is to enter a nunnery that day. Lucio is to ask Isabella to 'make friends / To the strict deputy'. Claudio describes Isabella as very persuasive, both in her appearance and in her use of argument. There is a subtext running through his choice of words, many of which are capable of a sexual interpretation, carrying a possible implication that Claudio expects that Angelo will be persuaded by Isabella's alluring intelligence and talents:

> for in her youth
> There is a prone and speechless dialect
> Such as move men; beside, she hath prosperous art
> When she will play with reason and discourse,
> And well she can persuade.   *(lines 163–7)*

Again Lucio's response to Claudio's poetic and elaborate imagery is in prose and is reductive. Claudio has spoken of his 'most mutual entertainment' with Juliet; in Lucio's terminology this becomes a 'game of tick-tack'.

Act 1 Scene 3

The Duke and Friar Thomas enter mid conversation. It appears that the friar has just made a suggestion, which the Duke is now denying (presumably that he has abandoned his position for the purpose of meeting a lover):

> Believe not that the dribbling dart of love
> Can pierce a complete bosom.   *(lines 2–3)*

The Duke seems to think of himself as being above falling in love, referring to Cupid's arrow as having lost its momentum ('dribbling') and saying that his intentions are more mature. He asserts that he has always valued a private and retired way of life. The Duke tells the friar that he has appointed Angelo as regent in his place, whom he describes as 'A man of stricture and firm abstinence', and that he has spread rumours that he himself has travelled to Poland.

As justification for such an extreme course of action, the Duke explains to the friar that though there are strict laws in Vienna, he has failed to enforce them. He compares himself to a father who has made a rod out of birch twigs, but has only hung it up to be a warning threat to his children; because they are never beaten, the children mock rather than fear the birch. The laws are ignored:

And Liberty plucks Justice by the nose,
The baby beats the nurse, and quite athwart
Goes all decorum. *(lines 30–2)*

Friar Thomas points out that it is the Duke's duty to enforce the law, but Duke Vincentio defends himself by claiming that it would seem 'tyranny' to allow the laws to lapse for years then suddenly enforce them. He explains that this is why he has appointed Angelo to be his deputy, to enforce the laws using the Duke's authority but without damaging the Duke's reputation. The Duke wishes Friar Thomas to lend him the garments of a friar and to coach him in the appropriate behaviour for a monk, so that he may stay in Vienna disguised to observe how Angelo rules. The Duke says that he will give Friar Thomas the reasons why he intends to do this later. The audience never hears these reasons, only the single one told here to Friar Thomas: that Angelo is 'precise' (observes a strict moral code) – he 'Stands at a guard with envy' (defends himself against any slander against his reputation) and 'scarce confesses / That his blood flows, or that his appetite / Is more to bread than stone' (he does not acknowledge that he has normal human passions and desires) – and the Duke wishes to see if he is changed by the acquisition of power:

Hence shall we see,
If power change purpose, what our seemers be. *(lines 54–5)*

Act 1 Scene 4

Again, Shakespeare begins the scene with the characters already talking. The implication of Isabella's opening question is that the Nun, Francisca, has been detailing the rules of the convent. As the Poor Clares had the reputation of being a very austere order of nuns, Shakespeare gives the audience an insight into Isabella's character by showing her requesting even more limitations on her freedom: 'a more strict restraint'. Her choice of words ironically reflects the situation of her brother, who is under a different kind of 'restraint' following 'too much liberty'.

Lucio calls from off stage, and Francisca explains a further rule of the convent: when they have taken their vows, nuns may only be in the company of a man when the prioress is present, and then they have to choose whether to speak to him unseen or to see him but remain silent. It is therefore Isabella, who has not yet taken her vows, who opens the door to Lucio. Typically, he shows a complete disregard for propriety by greeting her, 'Hail virgin', and he informs her that her brother is in prison. Still treating Claudio's offence as trivial, something for which he should be rewarded rather than punished, Lucio explains why Claudio has been arrested. When Isabella doubts him, he says that though his normal behaviour with women is to deceive them, he regards her as a saint because she has decided to renounce the world, and he is therefore being sincere. Isabella rebukes his exaggerated language. Lucio's euphemistic description of Juliet's pregnancy, which follows, is unusually lyrical:

> As those that feed grow full, as blossoming time
> That from the seedness the bare fallow brings
> To teeming foison, even so her plenteous womb
> Expresseth his full tilth and husbandry.   *(lines 41–4)*

Isabella guesses the identity of the woman immediately, which supports Claudio's claim of being informally married to Juliet. Her explanation that Juliet is 'Adoptedly' her cousin suggests that they have been close friends. Isabella's solution is simple: Claudio should marry Juliet. Lucio says that it is too late for that ('This is the point'), and explains that the Duke has disappeared, deceiving the people as to his intentions and his whereabouts. He tells her that the Duke has left Angelo in his place and has given him absolute power. Lucio describes Angelo as a man without passions:

> a man whose blood
> Is very snow-broth; one who never feels
> The wanton stings and motions of the sense   *(lines 57–9)*

Lucio says that Claudio is being made an example to demonstrate the newly enforced laws. He emphasises the speed of Angelo's judgement and encourages Isabella to plead for Claudio's life. Isabella doubts her ability to do anything to help, but Lucio persuades her, suggesting that young women can easily move men when they 'weep and kneel'. Isabella seems convinced, and says 'I will about it straight'.

> soon at night
> I'll send him certain word of my success.   *(lines 88–9)*

Act 1: Critical review

Act I is full of unanswered questions and parallels. The audience has to accept that the Duke is leaving in haste for an unknown reason and that Escalus, though the most experienced substitute, is being passed over. Angelo is the chosen deputy, but it seems to come as a surprise to him that he has been selected for such an exalted position. In the theatre the unanswered questions create a strong sense of dramatic tension.

Shakespeare juxtaposes the private, almost secretive scene of the Duke's departure with one of the few public scenes of the play. The Gentlemen and Lucio joke bawdily about their sexual experiences. Though the tone is comic as they make fun of one another, their language suggests decay and disease bought expensively at Mistress Overdone's brothel. As a swift consequence of Angelo's new authority, Claudio is arrested and paraded publicly through the streets, but his 'sin' seems healthy by comparison to Lucio and the Gentlemen. Claudio tells Lucio that his sister is about to enter a convent and asks him to persuade her to plead with Angelo on his behalf. Claudio's description of Isabella suggests that she has both intellectual and erotic power.

In another of the play's private scenes, the Duke denies that he has left the city because he has fallen in love. He tells Friar Thomas that he has left Vienna in the charge of Lord Angelo, 'A man of stricture and firm abstinence'. He describes Vienna as disordered and anarchic, a place where 'Liberty plucks Justice by the nose'. In the disguise of a friar, the Duke intends to test Angelo: 'Hence shall we see, / If power change purpose, what our seemers be.'

In the nunnery of the Poor Clares, Isabella is about to enter into her noviciate. Lucio, obeying his promise to Claudio, tells her of her brother's arrest. In keeping with his sympathetic attitude to Claudio's situation, he uses terms of natural fulfilment and harvest to describe Juliet's pregnancy. He persuades Isabella to attempt to use her power to reason with Angelo, 'a man whose blood / Is very snow-broth', who has decided to revive the old laws and to make an example of Claudio. Both Isabella and Angelo have now been taken from a 'life removed' and given responsibilities in the public sphere.

Act 2 Scene 1

Angelo and Escalus are discussing the newly enforced laws against fornication. On stage, Angelo opens the debate by saying that the law must be enforced or it will be ignored. Angelo's image of a scarecrow no longer feared by the birds echoes the Duke's image of a birch rod that is not feared by children in Act 1 Scene 3 (lines 24–7). Escalus responds with three separate arguments in defence of Claudio: first, he merely asks Angelo to be less extreme; second, he states that he knew and respected Claudio's father; third, he asks Angelo to consider whether he might, in certain circumstances, have thought about committing the same offence as Claudio. This last argument is to become one of the major themes of the play and is the only one to which Angelo responds:

> 'Tis one thing to be tempted, Escalus,
> Another thing to fall. *(lines 17–18)*

Angelo makes the point that there may be thieves in a jury that condemns a thief, but that this does not make wrong the sentence that they impose. He denies that Escalus' argument has any validity, claiming, ironically as it turns out, that were he ever to commit the same sin as Claudio then he should receive the same punishment without any special consideration:

> When I that censure him do so offend,
> Let mine own judgement pattern out my death
> And nothing come in partial. *(lines 29–31)*

Shakespeare reinforces the sense of the speed of Angelo's judgement by having him immediately instruct the Provost concerning the time of Claudio's death: 'See that Claudio / Be executed by nine tomorrow morning.' Escalus' reply, in rhyming couplets, is a series of *sententiae* (aphorisms or short sayings). The precise meaning is obscure and various editors have attempted to clarify the four lines by changing the spelling of some words. However, the general sense is clear: that some people can get away with sinning and others cannot.

The scene is then interrupted by the entrance of Elbow the constable, who is bringing in Pompey and Froth for judgement. The constable has a shaky grasp of English and confuses words, frequently giving the opposite meaning to his purpose: 'benefactors' for malefactors, 'detest' for respect, for example. His honest intention, but foolish inability to deal with the offenders is perhaps one reason for corruption being rife in Vienna; the power of the state depends upon the competence of its officers. Elbow has arrested Pompey and Froth, whom he calls 'precise villains'. 'Precise' is a word that has already been used to describe Angelo and it will be used about him again later in the play. It is not an appropriate word to use in relation to Pompey and Froth but it acquires a certain resonance from its misuse here. In his accusation of Pompey he also shows the consequences of Angelo's proclamation: Mistress Overdone's house has been 'plucked down' and she is now running a 'hot-house' or bathhouse, which is a cover for a brothel. Angelo's proclamation seems to have had little effect on the day-to-day running of the city.

Pompey tells a long and complicated story about Elbow's wife, involving a number of sexual innuendoes concerning prunes (see page 75). He is cunningly using an age-old technique of burying the exact details of his misdemeanours in a welter of irrelevant information: here, about the cost of the dish and the date of the death of Master Froth's father. His trick works, as Angelo becomes too irritated to continue listening to the evidence and leaves Escalus to hear the case. This could be interpreted as an echo of the Duke's abdication of power. Angelo also assumes the men are guilty, hoping that Escalus will 'find good cause to whip them all'.

Escalus makes an attempt to discover the true facts of the case but they are obscured by Pompey's constant distractions and by Elbow's malapropisms. In the event 'what was done to Elbow's wife' by Froth is left to the imagination of the audience. Pompey exploits the constable's misuse of language, leading Escalus to wonder, 'Which is the wiser here, Justice or Iniquity?' Escalus instructs Elbow to allow Pompey to 'continue in his courses' until he has concrete evidence of an offence. Elbow is pleased, assuming that this is Pompey's punishment. Shakespeare seems either to have had a particularly low opinion of the intelligence of constables, or they were easy targets for comedy. Escalus deals with each offender leniently, warning Froth to stay out of taverns.

Escalus makes a joke about Pompey's surname, Bum, with a probable reference to the fashion of his padded breeches. It is clear that Escalus does not believe Pompey's claim to be merely a 'tapster' (barman), and he warns him that he must stop being a 'bawd' (pimp). Pompey's defence is that the law is arbitrary (selling sex would be lawful if there were no law against it) and that sexual activity, especially amongst the young, is characteristically human. Escalus warns him that the laws concerning fornication are being enforced more rigorously, with infringements punishable by 'heading and hanging'. Pompey asks whether Escalus intends to castrate all the young people in the city, and says cynically that this law will radically diminish the population of Vienna. Referring to Caesar's defeat of Pompey, Escalus puns on Pompey's name and tells him that any further offence, however minor, will be severely punished. Pompey thanks Escalus for his warning, but makes it clear to the audience that he has no intention of reforming.

Escalus then turns to a possible root cause of the disorder by questioning Elbow about his role as constable. He discovers that when citizens are elected to do their term of office as constable of their parish, they pay Elbow to perform it for them. Escalus arranges to see the most 'sufficient' or able men in Elbow's parish the next day, presumably to stop them abusing the system (see page 64).

Escalus defends Angelo in his final conversation with the Justice, who has been silent on stage until this point. He refers to one of the themes of the play: that, in general, being merciful is not always the best course, which he balances with his sympathy for the particular case of Claudio. Ironically, this appears to be true in Pompey's case; he has been shown mercy by Escalus, but will continue to be a pimp.

> Mercy is not itself that oft looks so,
> Pardon is still the nurse of second woe.
> But yet, poor Claudio; there is no remedy.   *(lines 244–6)*

Act 2 Scene 2

The Provost goes to see Angelo in the hope that he will have reconsidered his decision. Like Pompey, the Provost considers Claudio's sin such a common offence that he should not be executed for it. Angelo seems angry at having his sentence queried and threatens the Provost coldly with dismissal. He instructs the Provost to move Juliet to a more suitable place to give birth: 'Dispose of her / To some more fitter place', calling her a few lines later the 'fornicatress'. Juliet is to be allowed what is necessary for her condition but not 'lavish' (extravagant) provision.

Isabella is announced and enters escorted by Lucio. Though the ensuing debate is between Angelo and Isabella, the Provost and Lucio are both present and, like onstage spectators, comment occasionally on the action, especially on Isabella's attempts to change Angelo's mind. Isabella has a difficult moral dilemma. She wishes to plead for her brother's life, but without making any suggestion that she approves of what he has done. Her language reflects the internal conflict she experiences:

> There is a vice that most I do abhor,
> And most desire should meet the blow of justice;
> For which I would not plead, but that I must,
> For which I must not plead, but that I am
> At war 'twixt will and will not.   *(lines 30–4)*

Her argument that Angelo should 'Condemn the fault', and not Claudio himself, is easily defeated by him. By definition the fault is already condemned. She recognises and accepts the force of this and turns to leave. Lucio persuades her to try again to 'entreat him', and tells her to kneel before Angelo. He tells Isabella that she is too 'cold' and must argue more forcefully:

> If you should need a pin,
> You could not with more tame a tongue desire it   *(lines 46–7)*

Her reasoning now centres on the need for Angelo to show mercy and on the Christian doctrine that Christ died to redeem sinners. Angelo adamantly refuses to be moved. She reminds Angelo that mercy is considered to be the most fitting attribute of the powerful, greater than the king's crown and other symbols of authority. She also claims that if the situation had been reversed, Claudio would not have been so severe, and she draws attention to Angelo's potential to be tempted:

> If he had been as you, and you as he,
> You would have slipped like him, but he like you
> Would not have been so stern.   *(lines 65–7)*

Angelo merely demands that she leave, but Isabella continues to press him to consider how it would be if their situations were reversed. As she is a novice, it is appropriate that Isabella's arguments should be based on Christian doctrine. She reminds Angelo of Christ's infinite mercy, and demands:

> How would you be
> If he, which is the top of judgement, should
> But judge you as you are? *(lines 77–9)*

Angelo denies a personal judgement: 'It is the law, not I, condemn your brother'. Again Shakespeare draws attention to the speed with which Claudio's execution will take place, as Angelo says, 'he must die tomorrow'. The suddenness of this seems to spur Isabella on to more forceful persuasion, asking for time for Claudio to be prepared for death. Isabella repeats an argument used by the Provost (at lines 4–6) and which will be echoed by others later in the play: that 'many have committed' the same offence as Claudio, and why should only he die for it? Lucio applauds her argument.

Angelo points out that fornication has always been against the law, even though punishment has not been enforced. He says that if the first person to offend in this way had been punished then it would have set an example to others, who would not have 'dared to do that evil'. In his personification of the Law he speaks of it as waking, seeing what the consequences of indulgence might be, and making a decision to prevent future offences. Like Escalus before her, in Scene 1, Isabella acknowledges the truth of his reasoning and can only ask for pity. Angelo responds with abstract, rather than personal justification: pity lies in justice. To punish a crime now is to show pity to unknown future generations by ensuring that the crime will not be committed in the future.

Isabella seems to become more angry and impassioned, possibly in response to his emotional detachment. She attacks Angelo personally in a long speech punctuated by encouraging asides from Lucio and the Provost. She accuses Angelo of arrogance and tyranny because he wants to use the power he has been given:

> So you must be the first that gives this sentence,
> And he, that suffers. Oh, it is excellent

> To have a giant's strength, but it is tyrannous
> To use it like a giant.   *(lines 109–12)*

In strongly sarcastic terms, Isabella claims that if man ('every pelting, petty officer') could wield power like the gods, there would never be any peace. She attacks the pride of mortal power by comparing it to that of 'Merciful heaven', which is used more sparingly and appropriately. Her image of 'man, proud man, / Dressed in a little brief authority', recalls the Duke's words from Act 1 Scene 1, line 19: 'Lent him our terror, dressed him with our love'. She derides man's confidence in the possession of a soul about which he knows nothing. She creates a memorably scornful picture of the petty judgements of 'proud man', who:

> like an angry ape
> Plays such fantastic tricks before high heaven
> As makes the angels weep; who, with our spleens,
> Would all themselves laugh mortal.   *(lines 124–7)*

When Angelo eventually interrupts to ask her, 'Why do you put these sayings upon me?' she says that 'authority' is also capable of sin but has a greater capacity to conceal it. Again Angelo is asked to assess his own conscience. Isabella says that if he can acknowledge this 'natural guiltiness' in himself, Angelo should not condemn Claudio:

> Go to your bosom,
> Knock there, and ask your heart what it doth know
> That's like my brother's fault.   *(lines 140–2)*

Earlier, at line 129, Lucio had noticed a reaction from Angelo. Now, in an aside, Angelo reveals to the audience that his emotions are stirred by Isabella, punning on the different meanings of 'sense' (reason and desire):

> She speaks, and 'tis such sense
> That my sense breeds with it.   *(lines 146–7)*

He turns away to leave her and Isabella begs him to turn back. Angelo gives her some hope by telling her to visit him 'tomorrow'. She shocks both him and Lucio with an offer to 'bribe' him, but Isabella is in fact offering to bribe Angelo with prayers. She uses two conventional phrases of leave-taking: 'Heaven keep your honour safe', and 'Save your honour', each of which Angelo interprets literally. To the first he replies, 'Amen' (so be it) because he is aware how much his desire for Isabella tempts him to sin, and to the second, 'From thee: even from thy virtue.'

In his soliloquy, Angelo reveals how appalled he is by how much Isabella sexually attracts him. In the first lines he almost seems to blame her ('Is this her fault, or mine?') but he goes on to show that he is very clearly aware that he is tempted to sin and that it is her virtue which has seduced him. He compares her to the sun, which shines on both flowers and dead flesh; the flowers are nurtured, but the flesh rots. Denying the truth of his own reasoning from Scene 1, lines 18–23, he now feels that he should let Claudio live, as 'Thieves for their robbery have authority / When judges steal themselves'. The whole soliloquy conveys a profound sense of the absolute shock experienced by Angelo that he has been attacked so suddenly and so completely by sexual desire:

> What, do I love her
> That I desire to hear her speak again
> And feast upon her eyes? *(lines 181–3)*

Shakespeare also gives the audience an insight into Angelo's inflated opinion of himself, as he terms himself a 'saint' tempted by another saint. He reflects on how, in the past, he could overcome all sexual temptation, but is now seduced by Isabella's virtues. He ends by declaring that until now he has never understood what makes other men fall in love.

> Ever till now
> When men were fond, I smiled, and wondered how.
> *(lines 190–1)*

Act 2 Scene 3

The Duke, now disguised as a friar, is visiting the prison and asks the Provost for permission to visit the prisoners to offer them spiritual counsel. The Provost's ready assent adds to the audience's impression of him as a sympathetic man: 'I would do more than that, if more were needful.' In speaking of Juliet, he describes her plight as a consequence of her youth. Claudio he describes as:

> a young man
> More fit to do another such offence
> Than die for this. *(lines 13–15)*

Shakespeare again reminds the audience of the speed with which Claudio's execution is to be carried out ('tomorrow'). The Provost tells Juliet that he has 'provided' for her, presumably according to Angelo's instructions. The Duke questions Juliet about her attitude to Claudio, to the sin and to her shame. She echoes Claudio's description of their 'most mutual entertainment' (Act 1 Scene 2, line 135) when she agrees that their offence was 'mutually committed'. The Duke alludes to the conventional idea of Shakespeare's time that makes the woman more culpable than the man: 'Then was your sin of heavier kind than his.' Juliet accepts the judgement, but the Duke wonders whether her repentance is caused by her sense of sin or whether it is merely because her pregnancy has made her crime public. Juliet interrupts him to assert that she repents the sin and carries the shame (her baby) 'with joy'.

When the Duke tells her that he is going to visit Claudio, he also abruptly informs her that Claudio is to die 'tomorrow'. The news shocks Juliet. Her reaction is one of distress that her pregnancy has saved her life but that she will have to live with the 'horror' of Claudio's death.

Act 2 Scene 4

Angelo is trying to pray, but while he speaks the words of the prayer he is thinking only of Isabella. He is all too aware of the contrast between the empty words of his prayer and his imagination, which is obsessed with Isabella's image:

> Heaven in my mouth
> As if I did but only chew his name,
> And in my heart the strong and swelling evil
> Of my conception. *(lines 4–7)*

Shakespeare gives Angelo a powerful image in this speech: of his merely mouthing the words of a prayer, or even perhaps of taking the Eucharist (the bread and wine taken at Mass), while the language gives a profoundly physical representation of Angelo's desire for Isabella. The word 'conception' is reminiscent of his senses 'breeding' in Scene 2, line 147. His former serious, puritanical interests have lost their attraction. He admits privately that he was proud of his 'gravity', but now feels that he would be prepared to exchange it for a more worldly reputation. He speaks of his consciousness that the outward forms of wealth and authority make the masses obedient, and that even those amongst them who are 'wiser' are deceived by 'false seeming'. 'Seeming' recalls the Duke's final lines of Act 1 Scene 3 and anticipates Isabella's reaction to Angelo later in this scene, at line 151.

Angelo is now forced to acknowledge that he is as human in his passions as other men; his statement 'Blood, thou art blood' reminds the audience both of the Duke's assessment that he 'scarce confesses / That his blood flows' (Act 1 Scene 3, lines 52–3), and of Lucio's more exaggerated view of him as a 'man whose blood / Is very snow-broth' (Act 1 Scene 4, lines 57–8). At the end of his soliloquy, Angelo acknowledges that it is impossible to disguise the true nature of evil: 'Let's write "Good Angel" on the devil's horn, / 'Tis not the devil's crest'.

When Isabella is announced, Angelo utters one of the most powerful descriptions of the effects of sexual desire:

> Oh, heavens,
> Why does my blood thus muster to my heart,
> Making both it unable for itself
> And dispossessing all my other parts
> Of necessary fitness? *(lines 19–23)*

He uses two further images in this personal and direct physical description of his feelings: that of a crowd depriving a fainting person of air by their over-eagerness to help, and that of the general public leaving their proper places to applaud their king, crowding him with their numbers (a probable reference to King James – see page 65).

The exchange between Angelo and Isabella which follows is this time in private, adding powerful dramatic effect to their uninterrupted dialogue. Isabella's greeting, 'I am come to know your pleasure', echoes Angelo's first words to the Duke in Act 1 Scene 1. Angelo gives her a sexually suggestive reply: 'That you might know it would much better please me / Than to demand what 'tis.' She accepts without question his statement that Claudio must die and turns to go. Angelo is forced to prevaricate in order to keep her there by suggesting that he might postpone the execution: 'Yet may he live a while'. Isabella shows that her concern is for Claudio's soul by asking Angelo to specify the time so that Claudio may prepare himself for death by confession and repentance.

Angelo suddenly breaks the flow of the discussion to repeat his disgust at fornication ('Fie, these filthy vices!'), but in his language he reveals his now more ambivalent attitude to sex. He says that the creation ('saucy sweetness') of illegitimate children is as sinful as murder, and as easy a sin to commit. Isabella agrees that they are both mortal sins but that society does not usually punish fornication with death. Angelo offers Isabella a choice based on her argument and again betrays to the audience his own confused feelings in the oxymoron 'sweet uncleanness':

> Which had you rather: that the most just law
> Now took your brother's life, or to redeem him
> Give up your body to such sweet uncleanness
> As she that he hath stained? *(lines 51–4)*

The bargain offered by Angelo is between Claudio's execution and Isabella's virginity but she does not fully comprehend his meaning, taking it as part of a hypothetical discussion. Isabella replies that she would rather die than commit a mortal sin, and the reference to her soul seems to irritate Angelo who wishes her to consider the question more carefully. In performance, Angelo's 'I talk not of your soul' often provokes audience laughter because, unlike Isabella, the audience knows that Angelo has only Isabella's body in mind. Using an argument to be echoed later by Claudio, he tells her that 'compelled sins' (forced wrongs) would not be held in judgement against her, though he immediately steps back from that point. He rewords his argument slightly more specifically:

> I, now the voice of the recorded law,
> Pronounce a sentence on your brother's life.

> Might there not be a charity in sin
> To save this brother's life? *(lines 61–4)*

Again Isabella misunderstands his darker meaning, interpreting the 'sin' mentioned at line 63 to be Angelo's leniency in pardoning Claudio, and she says she will accept the sin of begging for his life. Their words and phrasing echo one another's but are profoundly different in meaning:

ISABELLA Please you to do't,
> I'll take it as a peril to my soul,
> It is no sin at all but charity.
ANGELO Pleased you to do't, at peril of your soul,
> Were equal poise of sin and charity. *(lines 64–8)*

Angelo seems unsure if Isabella is being deliberately obtuse or 'crafty', though she denies it. He feels she is displaying a kind of false humility by drawing attention to her own lack of understanding. He says that, in order to make his meaning clear, he will 'speak more gross', first restating the fact of Claudio's crime and the justice of his sentence. Isabella accepts this, and for the third time Angelo offers her the choice. Though he has said that he will speak plainly, he still obscures his meaning with euphemisms; he does not mention himself but 'a person / Whose credit with the judge, or own great place' could secure Claudio's freedom, and he refers to the sexual act as laying down 'the treasures of your body'. Isabella now understands the nature of the bargain offered by Angelo but still sees it as part of a theoretical debate. Many critics see her reply as exposing hitherto unsuspected elements of her character. They feel that she reveals the kind of repressed sexuality displayed by Angelo, because in her reply there is a sharp contrast between form and content. Her denial is absolute but the language is very sensual and the imagery erotically physical:

> were I under the terms of death,
> Th'impression of keen whips I'd wear as rubies,
> And strip myself to death as to a bed
> That longing have been sick for, ere I'd yield
> My body up to shame. *(lines 100–4)*

Angelo's line in response is short (six syllables), 'Then must your brother die'; and Isabella matches it with another six-syllable line, 'And 'twere the cheaper way'. She goes on to make it clear that she is refusing because she thinks that she would suffer eternal damnation if she were to accept the bargain of her virginity for Claudio's life. Angelo asks her if she would not then be as severe as the law if she refuses an opportunity to save her brother. Isabella points out, in a doubly balanced set of images, that there is a great difference between a shameful ransom and freely offered pardon. Referring to her desperate pleading for Claudio's life in their last meeting, Angelo accuses her of diminishing the seriousness of his crime. Isabella still appears to think that she is taking part in an academic debate on the nature of Claudio's sin, and that the weakness of her argument has been exposed by Angelo:

> I something do excuse the thing I hate
> For his advantage that I dearly love. *(lines 120–1)*

Angelo's response, 'We are all frail' seems like a dryly sardonic comment on his own situation. Isabella suggests that if her brother's death were to result in the cessation of frailty, she would accept it. Angelo continues the theme of frailty, or weakness, and Isabella agrees that women are as frail and as easily broken as mirrors, and that men take advantage of their frailty. Angelo appears to be impatient and his tone becomes more imperative: 'Be that you are, / That is, a woman'. Isabella still does not understand his intentions and, again matching each other in two metrically short lines, Angelo tells her that he loves her; Isabella responds, 'My brother did love Juliet'. She still thinks that he is testing her virtue, but he insists that he is telling the truth: 'Believe me on mine honour, / My words express my purpose.' At this point in some modern productions, Angelo has physically assaulted Isabella, intending rape, and she has fought him off. Echoing his words 'honour' and 'purpose', Isabella accuses Angelo of 'seeming'. Her solution appears simple: he must pardon Claudio or she will tell the world of his hypocrisy.

Angelo's reply is chilling: 'Who will believe thee, Isabel?' He knows that his public reputation for austerity, and the fact that he is the Duke's chosen deputy, will make her accusation seem slanderous. Angelo uses an image of horses to imply that he is allowing his sensuality to take its own control: 'I give my sensual race the rein'. In a line full of aggressive consonants, he speaks of his 'sharp appetite'. For the first time he makes brutally clear the bargain he has already offered to her three times: 'redeem thy brother / By yielding up thy body to my will' or Claudio will not only die but suffer torture too. Again, the fact that she must give her answer 'tomorrow' gives the audience another reminder of the urgency and speed of the drama. Harshly, Angelo warns her that his position in the state will outweigh her innocence:

> Say what you can, my false o'erweighs your true.   *(line 171)*

Isabella is left alone on stage and desolately acknowledges the truth of Angelo's words: 'Did I tell this / Who would believe me?' She reflects that it is dangerous when those who represent the law are themselves corrupt, using their power to satisfy their desires. Isabella decides to go to her brother and, using a hyperbolic image, declares she is confident that even though his sin was provoked by sexual desire, he would rather die twenty times before he would allow his sister to be sexually corrupted. Isabella is threatened with rape; she intended to spend the rest of her life withdrawn from the world with her virginity devoted to God. At the end of her speech she measures the value of her virginity against that of her brother's life and many critics have hotly debated her decision:

> Then Isabel live chaste, and brother die:
> More than our brother is our chastity.   *(lines 185–6)*

Act 2: Critical review

Searching intellectual debates concerning law, justice and mercy all take place in Act 2. Pompey points out that the law is arbitrary: that his trade would be lawful 'If the law would allow it'. Isabella does not question the law in relation to her brother's guilt; she asks only for mercy. Angelo has to acknowledge the weakness of his own arguments in support of the law.

In a public hearing at the law courts, Escalus tries to persuade Angelo to pardon Claudio. He asks Angelo whether he might, under certain circumstances, have committed the same kind of sin as Claudio. Angelo points out logically that this is not the point: ''Tis one thing to be tempted, Escalus, / Another thing to fall', and that a crime cannot be excused because the judge might have committed the same crime. As though in rejection of Escalus' plea for mercy, Angelo specifies that Claudio must be executed 'tomorrow'.

The trial that follows concerns the low-life characters, where Pompey makes the point that unless all the young people in Vienna are castrated 'they will to't', and if everyone is executed who breaks the laws against fornication, Vienna will need repopulating after ten years.

The Provost feels that Angelo is being excessively severe to Claudio, as his crime is so common, and he comes to query the sentence. Angelo threatens him with dismissal. The Provost and Lucio provide an onstage audience for the first dialogue between Isabella and Angelo. Isabella appears to be as extreme as Angelo in her condemnation of Claudio's crime: 'There is a vice that most I do abhor, / And most desire should meet the blow of justice', though this contradicts her reaction in Act 1, 'O, let him marry her.' The intellectual power of Isabella's argument, and the passion with which she expresses it, stirs Angelo sexually: 'She speaks, and 'tis such sense / That my sense breeds with it.'

When Isabella returns to Angelo they are alone, and in a dramatically powerful episode he offers her Claudio's life in exchange for her virginity. Isabella refuses:

> Then Isabel live chaste, and brother die:
> More than our brother is our chastity.　　*(Scene 4, lines 185–6)*

Act 3 Scene 1

The Duke, in his disguise as a friar, visits Claudio in prison to offer him spiritual comfort. Claudio hopes that he will be pardoned, but says that he is 'prepared to die'. The Duke advises him to accept death stoically, 'Be absolute for death', and invites Claudio to engage in a metaphorical debate with life in order to convince him that life is not worth holding on to. Personifying life and death, he tells Claudio to consider that only a fool would want to keep life since it is subject to all that random fate can inflict upon it, and that death is inevitable and inescapable. He argues that Claudio cannot rely on his noble birth to save him because everything physical about him is ignoble and contemptible, and that he is not brave because he fears being eaten by worms. The Duke goes on to suggest that death is no more than sleep, which everyone finds desirable. In a reference to the biblical idea that man is made of earth, the Duke tells Claudio that he cannot even be sure of his own identity ('For thou exists on many a thousand grains / That issue out of dust'). He can never be happy because he is never satisfied with what he has. His personality is not fixed because his mood changes with the phases of the moon. Paradoxically his riches make him poorer because they take away his freedom; he is always bearing the heavy responsibility of his wealth, which anyway he cannot retain after death. Even his children will curse him for not dying more quickly. The Duke lists the ailments that afflict humanity and stresses the brevity of life:

> Thou hast nor youth nor age,
> But as it were an after-dinner's sleep,
> Dreaming on both   *(lines 32–4)*

Even if Claudio lives to be 'old and rich', he will not have kept his health, energy or looks. Finally the Duke asks him to consider what there is about this kind of existence that makes life worth living. He tells him that in life there are many deaths; however, even though it will end suffering, Claudio still dreads death. The Duke's catalogue of life's vanities and afflictions echo a theme much expounded upon in Shakespeare's time, *Ars Moriendi* ('The Art of Dying'), see page 62. Claudio has no answer to the Duke's philosophical reasoning and can only thank him for the advice:

> To sue to live, I find I seek to die,
> And seeking death, find life   *(lines 42–3)*

Isabella calls from off stage and says that she has come to visit Claudio. The Provost warmly invites her to enter. He speaks only three lines in this opening scene, but each confirms to the audience his kindly nature. He and the Duke then pretend to have business to discuss and 'conceal' themselves in order to overhear the conversation between Claudio and Isabella. Shakespeare shows Isabella's initial hesitation by giving her a one-word line, 'Why', suggesting a pause as she thinks about how to answer Claudio's first question. She begins by confirming to Claudio that he must die, though she tries to express it in as positive a way as she can by telling him that he must be Angelo's 'swift ambassador' to heaven. She asks him to prepare himself for his death 'Tomorrow'. Claudio asks her if there is any chance that he could be saved. Isabella's first word, 'None', dispels his hope, but she goes on to imply that there may be an alternative: 'such remedy as, to save a head, / To cleave a heart in twain'. This prompts Claudio to ask again, 'But is there any?' Isabella offers hope, but suggests that what she calls Angelo's 'devilish mercy' will grant Claudio his life but 'fetter you till death'. In an echo of Angelo's ambiguous phrasing in Act 2 Scene 4, Isabella avoids telling Claudio clearly what Angelo has suggested. She contrives to confuse Claudio whilst making her meaning clear to the audience. The audience can see that she means a spiritual and moral captivity, but Claudio assumes that she means life imprisonment. She seizes on his misapprehension and both confirms the idea of 'perpetual durance' and then complicatedly denies it by telling him that even if he were free to travel the whole world, his conscience would shame and restrain him. He asks her to clarify her meaning and Isabella suggests that it would be a loss of honour that he would suffer. Throughout this exchange Claudio's questions complete Isabella's lines, implying that he speaks urgently without leaving a pause after her speeches. He demands, 'Let me know the point.'

Isabella seems afraid to tell Claudio of Angelo's bargain, and says that she is worried that he may prefer to exchange a life of 'six or seven winters' for his enduring 'honour'. She asks if he is afraid to die, pointing out that the fear of death is worse than death itself. Claudio thinks that she doubts his courage and, in a sensual and physical image, speaks of embracing death:

> If I must die
> I will encounter darkness as a bride
> And hug it in mine arms.   *(lines 82–4)*

This kind of courageous affirmation seems to be what Isabella has been waiting for and she speaks of it approvingly, 'there my father's grave / Did utter forth a voice'. When she then describes Angelo as 'outward-sainted' and a 'pond as deep as hell', Claudio is shocked: 'The prenzie [precise, puritanical] Angelo?' Isabella finally tells him clearly that Angelo has offered to exchange Claudio's life for her virginity. His instant reaction is that Isabella should 'not do't'. Isabella says that she would be prepared to die to save him; her use of the expression 'As frankly as a pin' ironically echoes Lucio's words to her in Act 2 Scene 2, line 46:

> Oh, were it but my life
> I'd throw it down for your deliverance
> As frankly as a pin.   *(lines 103–5)*

Though Claudio thanks her for this empty offer, he begins to see hope of a reprieve. He moves gradually to consider fornication as the 'least' of the deadly sins, and that Angelo would surely not risk damnation for 'the momentary trick'. His change of mind is signalled bluntly: 'Death is a fearful thing.' Isabella's implacable resolve is equally evident in her reply, 'And a shamèd life a hateful.'

Claudio's speech, 'Ay, but to die' is a refutation of the Duke's coldly stoical 'Be absolute for death' argument (lines 5–41). Claudio's evocation of the physical effects of death, his references to his body, 'This sensible warm motion' and his 'delighted spirit', contradict all the abstract reasons given in the Duke's life-denying speech. Claudio's visions of Hell: 'fiery floods / . . . thrilling region of thick-ribbed ice' express the fearful ideas of what life after death would be like for those who had committed sin. His picture of being 'imprisoned in the viewless winds / And blown with restless violence round about / The pendent world' recalls the punishment of the illicit lovers, Paolo and Francesca, that Dante describes in *The Inferno*. Claudio's impassioned horror of death concludes with a direct reference to the Duke's list of all the disadvantages of life:

> The weariest and most loathèd worldly life
> That age, ache, penury, and imprisonment
> Can lay on nature, is a paradise
> To what we fear of death.   *(lines 129–32)*

Claudio begs Isabella to save his life, saying that the act of saving a brother's life changes sin to a virtue. Hysterically, she terms him 'beast', 'coward', 'wretch', and accuses him of 'a kind of incest'. She calls him perverted and says that she thinks that he is not her father's son. Violently she wishes death upon him, 'Take my defiance, / Die, perish', and says that she would not now take the smallest action to save him from death. Though he tries to interrupt her, she will not listen and, telling him that his sin was not an unpremeditated act but a 'trade' (linking him by implication to Pompey and the Viennese brothels), she says that allowing him to live would only lead to his committing further sexual misconduct. This virulent tirade of abuse is the last time she speaks to her brother in the play.

The Duke comes forward and asks Isabella to wait and speak to him. He tells Claudio privately that he has overheard what has passed between him and his sister, and that Angelo had only been testing Isabella's virtue and had not actually intended to corrupt her. He is in fact pleased that she had refused. The Duke claims to know this because he is Angelo's confessor. He warns Claudio that there is no hope of his being saved and that he must prepare himself: 'tomorrow you must die'. Claudio wishes to apologise to his sister and says he is ready for death. Shakespeare gives no stage directions here and directors can show by appropriate gestures whether they feel that Isabella rejects or accepts Claudio's apology. The Duke asks the Provost to take Claudio away and to leave him alone with Isabella, saying that her reputation will not be harmed by being left alone with a friar.

It is at this point in the play, at line 152, that some critics feel that the play changes in form and style. There is much less emphasis on the intellectual and emotional debates and a greater concentration on the working out of the plot. More of the lines are in prose and there are few extended images.

The Duke offers Isabella a compliment on her beauty and her virtue. He tells her that chance has revealed to him how Angelo has threatened her. He says that he would be more surprised at Angelo if there had not been so many other instances of men's 'frailty'. He asks her what she intends to do. Isabella has not changed her mind; she is going to tell Angelo that she will not submit to his desires. There is unconscious dramatic irony in her wish that she could tell the absent Duke about Angelo's betrayal of trust, and she says that if he does return she will tell him. The Duke agrees that, although it would be a good idea, at the moment Angelo could claim that he was only testing her virtue. He has a more positive plan to suggest. His idea will not only save her virtue and Claudio's life, but also it will help a 'poor wronged lady' and 'please the absent Duke' if he ever returns.

Isabella is eager to hear more and says she is willing to do anything that 'appears not foul in the truth of [her] spirit'. The Duke commends her courage and asks if she has heard of Mariana, whose brother died at sea. Isabella has, and knows that she had a reputation for virtue ('good words went with her name'). The Duke tells Isabella that Mariana had once been betrothed to Angelo, but before the marriage could take place, her brother's ship sank. Unfortunately he had with him Mariana's dowry (money which a woman brings to the marriage). Thus, in one accident, Mariana lost her brother, her fortune and her fiancé. Isabella is shocked that Angelo abandoned Mariana. The Duke confirms that Angelo 'Left her in her tears, and dried not one of them with his comfort', and adds that he also pretended to have discovered evidence of her immorality. Isabella feels that Mariana would be better dead, and that life itself must be corrupt to allow Angelo to continue living. The Duke explains that, against all reason, Angelo's cruelty has only increased Mariana's love. He instructs Isabella to go to Angelo, agree to his 'demands', but to stipulate that the time spent with him should be brief, with no words spoken and the place dark. When Angelo agrees to this, Mariana will take Isabella's place. If this 'encounter' becomes public it may force Angelo to marry her after all. The Duke claims that this plan will resolve all the present difficulties: Claudio will be saved, Isabella will not have to lose her virginity, Mariana may be helped, and Angelo will be tested. The Duke says that he will persuade Mariana if Isabella accepts his plan, and that the benefits justify the duplicity involved. Isabella readily agrees and the Duke instructs her to tell Angelo that she will accede to his desires, then to meet him (the Duke) at Mariana's home, 'the moated grange'.

Act 3 Scene 2

There is no necessary change of location as the Duke is already on stage. Elbow is bringing Pompey into the prison. He accuses him of buying and selling 'men and women like beasts' and, using an image taken from drinking, implies that Pompey's encouragement of fornication will result in a new race of bastards ('bastard' was a sweet Spanish wine). Pompey defends himself robustly, comparing the running of a brothel to money-lending. He claims that 'the merriest' of the two trades has been made unlawful, but that 'the worser' is legal and very profitable. He describes the wealthy usurer as wearing a gown lined with fox fur and lambskin, symbolising craft preying on innocence.

The Duke interrupts to ask why Pompey has been arrested. Elbow tells him, and says that he was also in possession of 'a strange picklock'. This can be seen as an ironic reference to the keys that Angelo will shortly give to Isabella to ensure her seduction. The Duke's angry condemnation of Pompey might seem hypocritical in relation to his eager plans for Mariana to be a substitute for Isabella. He demands that Pompey should cease earning his living from prostitution. Pompey tries to defend himself, but the Duke will not listen to a defence of sin. Significantly, the Duke's idea of the correct penalty for Pompey's vice is severe, but is not the extreme sanction imposed by Angelo on Claudio:

> Correction and instruction must both work
> Ere this rude beast will profit.   *(lines 29–30)*

Elbow says that Pompey is to be brought for judgement to Angelo, who has already given him a warning, though the audience knows that Angelo abandoned the last hearing and that it was Escalus who warned Pompey. The Duke closes the episode with an epigram that reminds the audience of other times when Angelo has been described as someone whose appearance does not match the reality of his character:

> That we were all, as some would seem to be,
> From our faults, as faults from seeming, free.   *(lines 34–5)*

Elbow expects that Angelo will order Pompey to be hanged and makes a macabre joke about Pompey's neck and the cord at the Duke's waist. Lucio enters and Pompey is relieved. He expects Lucio to stand bail for him. Lucio, however, exercises his wit at Pompey's expense, referring to the historic Pompey's capture by Caesar, and to the fact that he has no young whores with him. Lucio cynically teases Pompey with a series of questions, while the Duke comments bitterly on his levity: 'Still thus, and thus: still worse.' Lucio asks after Pompey's employer, Mistress Overdone, and Pompey describes her using contemporary slang expressions that are usually taken to mean that she is suffering from venereal disease. Lucio comments that this is an inevitable progression, from a young prostitute to an old 'powdered bawd'. When he hears that Pompey is going to prison, Lucio tells him to say that he sent him there, possibly suggesting that Lucio laid information against Pompey. He says if a prison is the punishment that a bawd should receive, then Pompey has earned it, and he jokes about Pompey having to be a 'good husband now' (he will have to stay indoors). Lucio again refuses to bail Pompey or help him in any way. Pompey's repeated requests for help suggest that Lucio is being disloyal by not helping him.

When Pompey and Elbow have left, Lucio asks the 'friar' for news of the Duke. The comedy of the following dialogue arises from the dramatic irony of the audience's knowledge that Lucio is speaking to the Duke himself. Lucio refers to the rumours about the whereabouts of the Duke. He criticises him for foolishly abandoning his rightful place and power and describes how 'Lord Angelo dukes it well in his absence' and how he punishes offences severely. When the 'friar' says briefly, 'He does well in't', Lucio comments that Angelo could be more lenient towards sexual transgression. The Duke says that sexual crimes are too common and 'severity' is the answer. Lucio agrees that it is a common vice, but says that fornication cannot be completely eliminated (echoing Pompey's earlier defence in Act 2 Scene 1, line 197). He compares sexual activity to the natural acts of eating and drinking. Mockingly he asks the Duke whether he agrees with the rumour that Angelo was not conceived in the usual way, but was born to a mermaid, or conceived by a pair of dried cod. He says that to his certain knowledge when Angelo 'makes water, his urine is congealed ice', and that he is a male puppet.

Lucio thinks that Angelo is without mercy to have a man executed for 'the rebellion of a codpiece'. He goes on to claim that the absent Duke would never have done such a thing because he was sexually promiscuous: 'he knew the service, and that instructed him to mercy'. The 'friar' is shocked by this slur upon his reputation and replies that the Duke was not interested in women, but Lucio insists that he knows best and describes the kind of woman the Duke frequented: 'your beggar of fifty'. He also accuses the Duke of drunkenness. Lucio claims to have been a close friend of the Duke, and that he knows the reason for his leaving the country but he will not tell, implying that it was for a disreputable cause. When Lucio tells the disguised Duke that he knows him to be a 'very superficial, ignorant, unweighing fellow' the Duke seems compelled to defend his own reputation. He accuses Lucio of speaking either from ignorance or malice, and claims that observing the way that the Duke had led his life must have made it clear that he was 'a scholar, a statesman, and a soldier'. Lucio maintains that he knows the Duke well and is speaking the truth. The 'friar' asks Lucio to tell him his name, so that if the Duke should ever return he would be able to call upon him to defend the stories he has just told. Confidently, Lucio tells his name and insists that he is prepared to say publicly what he knows of the Duke.

Changing the subject, Lucio asks the 'friar' whether it is true that Claudio is to be executed the next day. When the Duke asks why Claudio should die, Lucio replies with one of his euphemisms for sexual intercourse: 'For filling a bottle with a tundish [funnel]'. Again he says that he wishes the Duke were returned because Angelo is so severe he will depopulate the whole country by banning sex; even sparrows will be prohibited because they have a reputation for promiscuousness. He claims that this would never have happened if the Duke had not left: 'The Duke yet would have dark deeds darkly answered'. As he leaves, he once again slanders the Duke, saying that he would disobey the dietary rules of the Church ('would eat mutton on Fridays') and have sex with beggars. The Duke seems shocked and disturbed by Lucio's words and, alone on stage, meditates on the fact that no public figure can completely escape random malicious gossip however virtuous their life:

> No might nor greatness in mortality
> Can censure 'scape: back-wounding calumny
> The whitest virtue strikes.   *(lines 158–60)*

Escalus enters with Mistress Overdone and the Provost. She is begging to be granted mercy, but Escalus tells her she has been warned too often. Mistress Overdone claims that Lucio has given evidence against her, even though she has supported the child he has had by Kate Keepdown. Though the time since the Duke deputed Angelo to rule seems to have been no more than a few days, Mistress Overdone refers to Kate Keepdown as being pregnant during 'the Duke's time', yet now the child is almost a year and a quarter old. Shakespeare uses two time-schemes: one which is the emotional time of the threat to Claudio, and the other which is rarely mentioned but, as here, reflects realistic time.

Escalus has heard of Lucio as a promiscuous man and orders him to be brought for judgement. Mistress Overdone is taken off to the cells. Speaking to the Provost, Escalus says that he has tried unsuccessfully to persuade Angelo to rescind the order to execute Claudio, therefore Claudio should be given access to a priest. The Provost tells Escalus that the 'friar' has been visiting Claudio, and Escalus greets the 'friar', who says that he is visiting Vienna on 'special business' of the Pope. Escalus asks for news from abroad, and the Duke replies conventionally by saying that everything is getting worse. He then asks Escalus what the Duke's character was like, and Escalus gives a very different report of him from that given by Lucio: 'One that above all other strifes contended especially to know himself', 'A gentleman of all temperance'. The contrast between the louche Lucio and the sincere Escalus could not be more striking. However, Escalus is much concerned with Claudio's fate and with his readiness for death. The Duke says that he has spoken to Claudio, who accepts the justice of his punishment and, though he had hoped for deliverance, is now prepared to die. Escalus shows pity for Claudio's situation and again says that he has tried to persuade Angelo to be merciful, but has failed. There is marked irony in the Duke's remark that Angelo has sentenced himself if he should ever commit a similar crime. Unusually, Shakespeare gives the Duke a soliloquy in rhyming tetrameter couplets (four stressed feet in each line, instead of the five of pentameter, see pages 81–2). The different rhythm of the speech seems to be designed to draw attention to its function as a commentary on the action so far. The soliloquy contains a series of moral precepts, for example:

> He who the sword of heaven will bear
> Should be as holy, as severe   *(lines 223–4)*

The soliloquy can be divided into three sections. The first is general advice on the duties of a ruler who ought to live a blameless life (lines 223–8). It is followed by a condemnation of Angelo's particular conduct and hypocrisy (lines 229–38). Finally the Duke declares he will apply 'Craft against vice', and details his plan for the exchange of Mariana for Isabella:

> So disguise shall by th'disguised
> Pay with falsehood false exacting
> And perform an old contracting.   *(lines 242–4)*

Act 3: Critical review

Act 3 takes place entirely in the enclosed space of the prison. The central debate is between the absolutes of life and death. In a speech taken from a conventional list of philosophical consolations, the disguised Duke attempts to make Claudio prepared for his death. Later, when given the potential of life, even at the expense of his sister's shame, Claudio speaks of his terror of death in an emotional and physical rejection of the philosophy of the Duke's rational speech, concluding 'Sweet sister, let me live.'

At Scene 1, line 152, the style of the language of the play changes as the Duke begins to take an active role in the plot. There are fewer intensely poetic speeches, as prose takes over from verse. The Duke's speech, when alone with Isabella, about his plan to save her honour is in prose, and this marks the shift from the establishment of the plot to its resolution.

The audience is asked again and again in Act 3 to measure the actions of one character against another. Mariana still loves Angelo and the Duke plans that she should take Isabella's place, saving Claudio and possibly benefiting Mariana. The Duke claims that the ends justify the means: 'the doubleness of the benefit defends the deceit from reproof'. Pompey has been arrested again and the Duke rails at him for being a bawd. The depravity of Pompey's trade is balanced against the hypocrisy of Angelo.

Shakespeare precludes simple judgements of any of the characters: Lucio's betrayal of Pompey and Mistress Overdone is weighed against his loyalty to Claudio; Mistress Overdone's corruption as keeper of a brothel is balanced by her charity in maintaining the illegitimate child of Lucio and Kate Keepdown. Lucio's malicious gossip is measured against the judgement of Escalus and the actions of the Duke.

Unusually, the final speech in this act is in rhyming octosyllabic (tetrameter) couplets that make explicit the themes and issues of the play:

> He who the sword of heaven will bear
> Should be as holy, as severe   *(lines 223–4)*

Act 4 Scene 1

The location changes to Mariana's 'moated grange', where a boy is singing of a forsaken lover. The song reflects Mariana's situation and contrasts the faithlessness of the man with the desire of the woman. The change in tone is very marked as the wistful song and the single silent audience of Mariana contrasts vividly with the noisy prison scenes in the previous act. By the use of music, Shakespeare draws attention to the quiet and private life Mariana leads, away from the political turmoil of the city. When Mariana sees the 'friar' she instructs the boy to stop singing and to leave.

She describes the 'friar' as 'a man of comfort' and says that his advice has 'often' calmed her. This seems to emphasise Shakespeare's non-naturalistic use of timescale. While the realistic time for events such as the establishment of Angelo as the Duke's deputy and the 'plucking down' of the brothels must be fairly long, there is a parallel emotional time, stressing the brevity of the time available to Claudio. Again and again, Claudio is told that he must die 'tomorrow'. But Mariana implies here that she has known the 'friar' for some time and has confidence in him.

In a rhyming couplet, she apologises for the fact that the pleasure of music has alleviated her sorrow, in case the 'friar' thinks that she has been too merry. The Duke answers her in lines that have a similarly balanced structure as he argues that music has both good and bad effects. He changes to prose to ask Mariana if anyone has called asking to see him. Mariana is just saying that there has been no one when Isabella arrives. The Duke asks Mariana to wait aside, saying that he may be able to give her good news soon, and she leaves the stage.

Isabella launches immediately into an account of the arrangement that she has made with Angelo, who has planned a very private rendezvous with her. He has given her two keys so that she can let herself into the vineyard and from there into his garden. She is to meet him there in the middle of the night. He had explained and shown the way to her twice, 'With whispering and most guilty diligence'. The Duke asks if there are any other signs that they have agreed on. Isabella says there is nothing else, but that she has warned Angelo that she can only make a short stay, and that there will be a servant with her who thinks she has come to plead for her brother.

The Duke says that the plan has been well arranged. He now introduces Isabella to Mariana. He asks Mariana if she trusts him.

When she says that she does, he asks her to listen to what Isabella has to tell her. He tells them to hurry as 'night approaches'. To avoid repetition, Shakespeare has the conversation between Isabella and Mariana take place either aside or, in some productions, completely off stage, while the Duke has a six-line meditation on the fact that public figures have no privacy and are the subject of slanderous rumours: 'Oh place and greatness, millions of false eyes / Are stuck upon thee'. Very quickly Mariana agrees to take Isabella's place, if the 'friar' should 'advise it'. The Duke entreats her to agree to it. Isabella gives some words of advice and Mariana is prepared to go. In the final lines of the scene the Duke draws attention to the fact that Angelo and Mariana have been contracted to marry and that therefore the consummation of their betrothal is not a sin:

> Come, let us go,
> Our corn's to reap, for yet our tithe's to sow.   *(lines 72–3)*

Act 4 Scene 2

The location changes back to the prison and the tone to comedy. The action of the scene takes place during the night. The Provost asks Pompey to become the assistant executioner. Pompey has a choice of sorts: to accept the post, which will shorten his sentence in jail; or to refuse, stay imprisoned for the full term and be whipped before he is released. Not surprisingly, Pompey rapidly agrees to be a 'lawful hangman' as a change from being an 'unlawful bawd'. The Provost calls the executioner, Abhorson, to see Pompey, who is to assist him in the beheading of Claudio and another prisoner, Barnardine, 'tomorrow'. If Abhorson is satisfied with Pompey's work during the next morning, the Provost tells him to settle how much he will pay him; if not, then Abhorson can dismiss him. Pompey cannot complain as he is in prison for being a pimp. Some of the comedy derives from the way that Abhorson (a name compounded of 'abhorrent' and 'whoreson') is shocked that he is expected to have a bawd as his assistant. He says that Pompey will 'discredit our mystery', claiming by the use of the word 'mystery' that being a hangman is a skilled trade and that he is part of a guild. The Provost has little patience with the argument and seems to be contemptuous of both men: 'Go to, sir, you weigh equally: a feather will turn the scale.'

When the Provost has left, Pompey questions Abhorson about his reasons for calling hanging a 'mystery'. Pompey claims that being a bawd has more justification to the term, as painting is a 'mystery' and prostitutes paint their faces. Abhorson's defence of his profession is confusing, but he at least seems convinced by it.

When the Provost returns, Pompey says he will work with Abhorson, and Abhorson is instructed to prepare his block and axe for 'tomorrow' (Shakespeare seems to make no distinction between hanging and beheading). Pompey and Abhorson leave the stage with Pompey saying, 'if you have occasion to use me for your own turn, you shall find me yare [ready]', a typical example of Pompey's wit, which ambiguously suggests either that he will be ready to help Abhorson, or that he will be ready to execute him. The Provost asks them to send Claudio and Barnardine to him.

In the brief time that the Provost is alone on stage, he expresses pity for Claudio, but none for Barnardine because he is a murderer. Claudio joins him almost immediately and the Provost shows him his death warrant: ''Tis now dead midnight, and by eight tomorrow / Thou must be made immortal.' Claudio makes no spoken response to this and the Provost asks him where Barnardine is. Claudio tells him that Barnardine is sleeping like an innocent hardworking man. The news prompts the Provost to wonder if anyone can 'do good' to Barnardine. As the Provost is advising Claudio to prepare himself for death there is a knock at the door of the prison. He hopes that it is a 'pardon or reprieve / For the most gentle Claudio'.

The Duke enters, still disguised as the friar. He clearly expects that the Provost will soon receive a reprieve for Claudio from Angelo as a result of Mariana's visit to his garden. The 'friar' defends Angelo from the Provost's accusation of cruelty by saying that Angelo's life clearly demonstrates that he is of ascetic character, conquering in himself the sexual desire he seeks to restrain in others:

> He doth with holy abstinence subdue
> That in himself which he spurs on his power
> To qualify in others. *(lines 68–70)*

The Duke says that it would be different if Angelo had the same faults as those he punishes; then he could be called 'tyrannous', but as he does not have these faults, 'he's just'.

There is another knock at the door, and the Provost leaves. The Duke expects that word has come from Angelo. He comments on the fact that the Provost is unusually kindly for a man in charge of a prison. When the Provost returns, the Duke asks if he has received any reprieve for Claudio, and he makes it clear that he expects a message before morning. Although the Provost is prepared to believe that the 'friar' knows more than he does, he doubts whether there will be any such message, as there is no precedent for it and Angelo has made his decision in relation to Claudio very public. When the messenger enters, the Duke is convinced that 'here comes Claudio's pardon'. The messenger warns the Provost that Angelo instructs him to obey the message precisely. As he leaves, he increases the tension by remarking that 'it is almost day'. While the Provost reads the message sent by Angelo, the Duke comments in rhyming couplets on what he takes to be the contents:

> This is his pardon, purchased by such sin
> For which the pardoner himself is in.   *(lines 94–5)*

He thinks that Angelo's own sin will have instructed him to be merciful. The Provost dispels this conviction by telling the 'friar' that Angelo has merely ordered that Claudio be executed promptly in the morning and the head sent to Angelo as proof that he is dead. Barnardine is to be executed in the afternoon.

The Duke asks who Barnardine is, and is told that he is from Bohemia and has been in prison for nine years. The Duke asks why he has not been released or executed before this. The Provost accounts for the delay by saying that not only did Barnardine's friends plead for him, but also there was no absolute proof of his guilt until recently. Barnardine does not deny his guilt and he is described as:

> A man that apprehends death no more dreadfully but as a
> drunken sleep: careless, reckless, and fearless of what's past,
> present, or to come   *(lines 125–7)*

The Provost says that he has had the run of the prison and the freedom to escape, but that he spends most days drunk. The Provost has shown him a fake death warrant but even this has not disturbed him. It appears Shakespeare is encouraging the audience to develop an ambivalent attitude to Barnardine: either admiration for his casual attitude to death, or lack of sympathy for his reckless behaviour. The Duke asks the Provost to wait for four days before the execution. The Provost refuses on the grounds that Angelo would execute him if he were to delay. The Duke's solution is that Barnardine should be executed straight away and his head sent to Angelo instead. The Provost points out that they are unlike each other and Angelo has seen them both. The Duke rather desperately claims that 'death's a great disguiser', and that if Barnardine's head is shaved and his beard is trimmed Angelo will never know the difference. The Provost continues to refuse, and the Duke has to take the further step of showing the Provost a paper with his handwriting and ducal seal. He says that the letter concerns the return of the Duke within two days, and that Angelo does not know this. On the contrary, Angelo has received confusing letters which imply that the Duke may have died or entered a monastery. He leads the Provost off stage, saying that he must hear Barnardine's confession before he dies. He says that the letter will make everything clear to the Provost. He insists on haste:

> Come away, it is almost clear dawn. *(lines 182–3)*

Act 4 Scene 3

Still in the prison, Pompey has a typical 'clown' speech that would probably have been addressed to the audience, embarrassing particular individuals. He implies that the people he can see in front of him are his fellow prisoners and old acquaintances from his days in Mistress Overdone's brothel. He details some of the stock types of Jacobean society, many of whom he describes as imprisoned for debt or for violence. Abhorson tells him to fetch Barnardine and make him ready for execution, but Pompey's attempts to raise Barnardine are unsuccessful. He refuses to be executed because he is too sleepy. Pompey tells him he can be executed first and sleep afterwards. Eventually Barnardine comes on stage, but he refuses to be executed because he has been drinking all night and is not 'fitted for't'. His words parody Isabella's concern that her brother should have time to make himself ready for death. The 'friar' enters and rather pompously tells Barnardine that he has 'come to advise [him], comfort [him], and pray with [him]'. He is disconcerted by Barnardine's brusque refusal and has to resort to almost begging Barnardine to be executed.

Barnardine refuses to listen to the Duke and leaves the stage. He says that if the friar has anything more to say to him then he will have to say it in his cell, because he is not coming out of it again that day. The Duke is forced to send Pompey and Abhorson after him to 'bring him to the block'.

The Duke's plan seems to be going wrong. He feels that it would be a sin to execute Barnardine in his present state of mind. However, the Provost has news that resolves the dilemma. By chance, another prisoner, Ragozine, has died of a fever and he is luckily of a similar height and colouring to Claudio. He also happens to be a convicted pirate, so the audience does not have to feel pity for his death. Ragozine's head can be cut off and sent to Angelo in place of Claudio's. The Duke says that ''tis an accident that heaven provides', often provoking laughter in the theatre. He tells the Provost to see that it is done immediately as the time set by Angelo is approaching, while he tries to persuade Barnardine to die willingly. The Provost continues to worry about Angelo finding out that Claudio is still in the prison, and the 'friar' suggests that Barnardine and Claudio are each put in separate secret cells for the next two days until the Duke returns. The Provost leaves the stage to arrange for Ragozine's head to be sent to Angelo.

Alone on stage, the Duke reveals the latest stage in his plans. He is going to write to Angelo to tell him that he is returning and that he will make a public entry to the city. He will arrange to meet Angelo at a holy well just outside the city and will then by degrees bring Angelo to justice. The Provost returns with Ragozine's head and says he will take it himself to Angelo. The Duke asks him to return quickly because he has something to say to him.

As the Provost leaves, Isabella's voice is heard off stage. Before she enters, the Duke tells the audience that he will keep secret the fact that Claudio has not been executed: 'To make her heavenly comforts of despair / When it is least expected'. The Duke's seemingly cruel decision has provoked much critical debate. Isabella greets the 'friar' and asks if her brother's pardon has arrived from Angelo. Concealing the plot he has made to deceive Angelo and save Claudio, the Duke tells her directly that Claudio has been executed. Isabella is shocked and horrified by the news and says she 'will to him and pluck out his eyes'. She rails at Angelo's treachery and the Duke tries to calm her: 'This nor hurts him nor profits you a jot.' He tells her to listen to his advice, and that what he speaks will be a 'faithful verity'. He says that the Duke will return 'tomorrow', breaks off to comfort her ('nay, dry your eyes'), then reports that Escalus and Angelo have already had the news. They have been instructed to meet the Duke at the gates of the city to relinquish their power. He advises her that if she can have the patience to obey his instructions then she will be revenged on Angelo, please the Duke and maintain her reputation. In a brief acknowledgement of her obedience, Isabella says she will do as he asks. He gives her a letter to Friar Peter to ask him to meet the 'friar' at Mariana's house 'tonight'. He will explain Isabella's story to Friar Peter, who will accompany her to accuse Angelo. The Duke tells her that he cannot be there on the next day as he is constrained to be elsewhere by a 'sacred vow'. Again he tells her to stop weeping and to trust him.

Lucio enters, looking for the Provost. In a number of modern productions he has evoked audience laughter by expressing mock prurient surprise at finding the 'friar' and Isabella alone together. He shows some pity for Isabella's distress, but typically declares that he is taking care not to eat anything that may arouse him sexually in case he finds himself in the same situation as Claudio. He has also heard the news that the Duke is returning and derisively asserts that if 'the old fantastical Duke of dark corners' had been in Vienna earlier, Claudio would not have been executed. Isabella leaves the stage without replying, and the 'friar' tells Lucio that the Duke would give him little gratitude for his comments on his character, but that fortunately the picture he paints is nothing like the Duke. Lucio claims that his knowledge of the Duke is better and that Vincentio is more of a womaniser than the friar realises. The Duke warns Lucio that one day he will answer for what he has said and tries to leave but Lucio insists that he will accompany him and tell him more gossip about the Duke. The 'friar' says that Lucio has already said too much. Lucio reveals that he was once brought before the Duke, charged with getting a woman pregnant. It was true, though he denied it because he did not want to have to marry the girl, whom he terms a 'rotten medlar'. Again the Duke tries to leave him, but Lucio, with his typically sardonic humour, insists on going with him and they leave the stage together:

> If bawdy talk offend you, we'll have very little of it. Nay, friar,
> I am a kind of burr, I shall stick.   *(lines 163–5)*

Act 4 Scene 4

Escalus and Angelo are discussing the confusing letters they have received from the Duke. They say that each new letter contradicts the previous one, and that they are worried that the Duke has lost his wits. They query the fact that the Duke has instructed them to meet him at the gates of the city to relinquish their power. They also wonder why the Duke has instructed them to send out a proclamation to inform anyone who has a grievance against their rule that they should announce it there. Escalus says that he understands the Duke intends to deal with any complaints then so that no accusations can be made against them later. Angelo instructs Escalus to deal with the proclamation and to inform other men of rank to meet the Duke in the morning.

Escalus leaves and, alone on stage, Angelo reveals his guilt and disturbance. He is appalled by his actions during the previous night and his language is full of sexual overtones:

> A deflowered maid,
> And by an eminent body that enforced
> The law against it?   *(lines 19–21)*

He is aware that because he has a reputation for integrity and his place in the state carries such credit, no one can accuse him without the scandal rebounding on themselves. He knows he should have allowed Claudio to live, but he was afraid that Isabella would have told her brother, who might have taken revenge for her rape. Ironically, the language he uses reflects Isabella's tirade against her brother's plea for life in Act 3 Scene 1. Angelo shows regret for what he has done, but little remorse.

> Would yet he had lived.
> Alack, when once our grace we have forgot,
> Nothing goes right: we would, and we would not.   *(lines 30–3)*

Act 4 Scenes 5 and 6

In the brief Scene 5 the Duke is no longer disguised as a friar and gives instructions to Friar Peter. Scene 6 is also a very short scene, again increasing the sense of dramatic speed. Isabella and Mariana are discussing the instructions left for them by the 'friar'. Isabella is reluctant to conceal the truth. She would prefer that Mariana should accuse Angelo, but the 'friar' has advised her to do so. Mariana seems to have complete faith in him and counsels Isabella, 'Be ruled by him.' The disguised Duke has also warned her that he may speak against her, but that she is not to consider that 'strange' because the positive ends will justify any difficulties she may experience. Shakespeare heightens the dramatic tension by having Mariana say that she wishes that Friar Peter would come just at the moment he enters. He tells the women that the Duke is on his way and the dignitaries of the city are already at the gates to greet him.

Act 4: Critical review

There are several short scenes in Act 4, each progressively emphasising the speed of the action. They take place in intense enclosed spaces: the grange, which is 'moated', suggesting that it is protected or defended; the prison; Angelo's study; a monastery.

At Mariana's 'moated grange', a boy is singing a wistful love song, contrasting with the noisy, bawdy action at the prison. With the entrance of the Duke, the tone becomes more urgent. The agreement of Mariana to the Duke's plan is obtained speedily. The return to the sub-plot of Pompey's new job as hangman's assistant lowers the tension briefly and reminds the audience of social realities. There is humour as Abhorson and Pompey have a mock debate about the merits of their trades, which is interrupted by the Provost. Through the rest of this scene the time is mentioned frequently, marking the passing of the night as the Duke first awaits Claudio's pardon, then plans the alternatives: 'midnight . . . eight tomorrow . . . tomorrow . . . near the dawning . . . almost day . . . four of the clock . . . five . . . almost clear dawn'.

Again it is Pompey who reduces the tension with his conventional clown's speech to the audience, setting the context of the play firmly in Shakespeare's London. Barnardine's refusal to be hanged because he is too drunk also adds potential humour and illuminates Isabella's earlier concern over Claudio's preparedness for death. Barnardine almost seems like a plot device – he is going to be executed anyway; he freely admits his guilt and has few redeeming qualities, but Shakespeare makes it clear that even a life like Barnardine's must be respected. His life cannot be cut short just to benefit Claudio. The unfortunate Ragozine, who dies by chance in prison 'of a cruel fever', becomes the convenient substitute, and again the speed of the action is compressed. When Isabella arrives, the Duke as friar untruthfully tells her that Claudio is dead but that she should demand justice from the returning Duke. Isabella's grief is balanced by the dramatically ironic comic patter of Lucio, still insistently slandering the Duke.

The final three scenes are very brief and the location changes in each. These scenes prepare for the denouements to take place at the city gates of Vienna.

Act 5 Scene 1

This act takes place at the gates of the city of Vienna, where the Duke is formally greeting Escalus and Angelo. It is a public scene with many 'extras': lords, citizens and officers. It can be a challenge to a director to manage a large number of non-speaking actors on stage while keeping the attention of the audience on the main characters. It makes a striking contrast to the many enclosed and private scenes of the play, and also symbolises that the revelation of Angelo's hypocrisy will take place in full public view: it is a political event.

The Duke speaks with the royal 'we' as he thanks both Escalus and Angelo for their good offices while he was away. There is an implicit warning to Angelo, 'We have made enquiry of you', and though the Duke says that he has heard, 'Such goodness of your justice', he also cautions, 'Forerunning more requital' (anticipating greater rewards – or retribution – for Angelo). Angelo not only replies to the surface meaning of the Duke's words when he says, 'You make my bonds still greater' (your thanks make me even more aware of what I owe you as a subject), but the audience recognises in his words a covert reference to his sense of undeserving.

The Duke continues with fulsome praise of Angelo's merits and says that they deserve a public lasting memorial. He takes Angelo's hand to demonstrate to the assembled citizens how much he values him. The Duke asks Escalus to walk beside him on his other side. As they process into the city, Friar Peter prompts Isabella to speak out and kneel before the Duke. She calls for 'Justice' and speaks of herself as a wronged 'maid' or virgin. She asks him to consider her case before he enters the city. She cries insistently for

> . . . justice, justice, justice, justice!   (line 25)

The Duke says that she should explain how she has been wronged, and tells her that 'Lord Angelo shall give you justice'. Isabella is appalled: 'You bid me seek redemption of the devil', and she asks the Duke to hear her case himself, as either his disbelief will be her punishment or he will avenge the harms she has suffered. Her passion is once again expressed with vehement repetition: 'Hear me, oh hear me, here!'

During the following exchanges, Shakespeare employs further rhetorical devices to emphasise the strength of Isabella's demands.

Angelo begins by suggesting that Isabella is unstable because she has been unsuccessfully pleading for her brother's life, 'Cut off by course of justice'. Isabella interrupts to echo, 'By course of justice!', but Angelo continues to prepare the Duke for Isabella's unlikely accusations by warning him that she will 'speak most bitterly and strange'. Isabella picks up Angelo's word 'strange' and uses it five times in the next six lines. She says that she is speaking the truth and asks if it is not 'strange' that Angelo should be a liar, a murderer, a thief, a hypocrite and a rapist. Her questions have a powerfully persuasive force in their patterned repetition. In response, the Duke comments dryly that it is 'ten times strange'. Isabella now asserts the truth of her claim: it is 'as true as it is strange', and hammers out the veracity of her accusations:

> Nay, it is ten times true, for truth is truth
> To th'end of reck'ning.   *(lines 45–6)*

The Duke rejects her plea and orders that she should be taken away. He claims to think that she has lost her wits. Isabella pleads her case, desperately begging him, as he has faith in the existence of heaven, not to assume that she is mad, just because what she is saying seems incredible. She argues that a villain 'May seem as shy, as grave, as just, as absolute / As Angelo' (lines 54–5) and that, in spite of his appearance, Angelo is a complete villain; if she could think of a more extreme word for evil she would use it to describe him. The Duke comments that though he is sure she is mad, her speech has more logic and structure than that of many sane people. Isabella becomes worried that the Duke appears too prone to believe that she is mad. She asks him to:

> let your reason serve
> To make the truth appear where it seems hid,
> And hide the false seems true.   *(lines 65–7)*

Her stress on 'seems' recalls the many times in the play that Angelo has been linked to the words 'seem' and 'seeming' and to the theme of appearance and reality. The Duke comments that more confusion is often shown by those who are sane, and he gives her permission to speak.

Isabella begins to explain her situation relatively dispassionately. Lucio interrupts and tells of his own contribution to the attempts to save Claudio's life. The Duke rebukes him sternly, 'You were not bid to speak.' Lucio acknowledges this, but typically adds he has no wish to be silent. Shakespeare makes the Duke's feelings towards Lucio clear when he instructs him again to be silent, but to be ready to answer for himself when the time comes. Lucio replies with the conventional, 'I warrant your honour', but the audience is aware of the alternative meaning of warrant (for arrest) in the Duke's reply, 'The warrant's for yourself'. It seems that Shakespeare is not only using Lucio to reduce the tension here and to remind the audience that he intends a satisfactory result for Isabella, but also comically to prepare for Lucio's eventual downfall.

Isabella is interrupted again by Lucio, and a further time by the Duke, who warns her against using extreme language ('pernicious caitiff') to describe Angelo. She finally completes her account of the sexual bargain made with Angelo. Obedient to the 'friar's' instructions, she lies and says that she gave in to Angelo's demands: 'I did yield to him'. She tells how Angelo nevertheless had Claudio executed once he had satisfied his desires.

The Duke says that he does not believe her story, though Isabella claims that it is true. He accuses her of either being mad or that she has been bribed to denounce Angelo, and that there are two reasons why her accusation must be false: one is that Angelo's reputation is stainless; the other is that it would be hypocritical of Angelo to punish someone so severely for faults that he had himself committed.

> If he had so offended,
> He would have weighed thy brother by himself
> And not have cut him off. *(lines 110–12)*

These lines echo the many times Angelo has been asked to consider whether in certain circumstances he might be tempted to sin like Claudio. The Duke claims to be convinced that someone else has persuaded Isabella to accuse Angelo and he asks her to confess that this is so and to say who has bribed her to do it.

Isabella is appalled that she is not believed and, asking heaven to keep her patient and to reveal the truth in the future, she says she is leaving. The Duke orders her arrest because she has slandered someone holding such high office. He declares it must be a plot and asks who knew that she intended to accuse Angelo. Isabella replies that 'Friar Lodowick' knew, giving the Duke's alias for the first time in the play. The Duke accuses her of inventing the existence of the friar, 'A ghostly father, belike', and asks who else knows of him. Lucio claims acquaintance with the friar, and says that if Lodowick had not been in holy orders he would have thrashed him for insulting the absent Duke. The Duke expresses surprise, 'Words against me?', and pretends to believe Lucio's account. Again, Shakespeare is deliciously building up the comedy and irony that will add to the audience's enjoyment of Lucio's eventual exposure. The Duke suggests that this 'friar' suborned Isabella and asks for him to be brought before him. Lucio says he saw the 'friar' and Isabella at the prison the previous night, and implies that there was sexual mischief between them: 'a saucy friar'.

Friar Peter now interrupts and accuses Isabella of lying when she charges Angelo with violating her honour. The Duke replies that he never doubted Angelo, and asks if Friar Peter knows of Friar Lodowick. Friar Peter, challenging Lucio, asserts that Friar Lodowick is 'a man divine and holy', who would not have insulted the Duke. Lucio bluntly maintains his lie, declaring that he is speaking the truth about the friar. Friar Peter says Friar Lodowick would be able to defend himself but that at present he is ill. Because Friar Lodowick had information that Angelo was to be accused, he has asked Friar Peter to come on his behalf to defend Angelo from any accusation that he had sexual relations with Isabella and to produce a witness to prove that she is lying.

It is not clear quite when Isabella leaves the stage, or why she remains silent, but she is not present for the next part of the scene (some editors insert a stage direction that she is led off, guarded). The Duke invites Friar Peter to continue, and asks Angelo if he is not amused by these false accusations. He invites Angelo to take his place once more, and to judge the case for himself. Mariana enters, veiled, and the Duke asks if this is the witness and for her to show her face. Mariana refuses, saying that she will only show her face if her husband asks her. In a riddling series of replies to the Duke's questions, Mariana denies that she is married, a virgin or a widow, prompting the Duke to declare:

> Why, you are nothing then: neither maid, widow, nor wife?
>
> *(line 177)*

Lucio cannot resist interjecting that she may be a prostitute. The Duke asks for him to be silenced, and Mariana reveals a little more: that she is not married and not a virgin because she has had sexual intercourse with her husband, though her husband is unaware of the fact. To the Duke's increasing annoyance, Lucio again interrupts, asserting that the husband must have been drunk at the time.

The Duke asks how Mariana's information can help to defend Angelo from slander, and she replies that her husband is also accused of fornication by Isabella but at a time when she (Mariana) will swear that he was making love to her. Angelo speaks for the first time since line 36 to ask whether Isabella lays this charge to any other man. Mariana tells him that Isabella only accuses her husband and that he is Angelo, who thinks that he has not known her (Mariana) sexually but thinks that he has had sexual relations with Isabella. Angelo instructs Mariana to show her face, and she obeys:

> My husband bids me, now I will unmask.
> This is that face, thou cruel Angelo,
> Which once thou swor'st was worth the looking on.
>
> *(lines 203–5)*

Rhetorically she repeats the phrasing 'This is . . .': 'This is that face . . . This is the hand . . . This is the body'. She concludes with the information, new to Angelo, that she took Isabella's place in his 'garden-house'.

The Duke asks Angelo whether he knows Mariana, and Lucio interrupts with another quip, punning on the idea of carnal (sexual) knowledge. The exchange between the irritated Duke and Lucio also gives time for Angelo to react and think. He admits that he knows Mariana, and that five years previously there had been talk of marriage, but he claims that it was broken off, partly because she had less money than they had agreed on, but mainly because he discovered that she did not have a good reputation. Angelo says that he has not been in contact with her since.

Mariana's version is different. She says that she is betrothed to Angelo 'as strongly / As words could make up vows'. She also affirms that she had sexual intercourse with Angelo in his garden-house (for Jacobean attitudes to consummation after betrothal, see pages 67–9). At some time during or just before her speech, Mariana must have knelt before the Duke because here she says that if she is speaking the truth she will be able to rise, but if she is lying she will remain fixed on her knees, like a marble statue.

Referring to the Duke's question (line 163), and recalling for the audience his comment in Act 2 Scene 2, lines 190–1, Angelo says, 'I did but smile till now.' He asks the Duke to allow him the full extent of justice, a request charged with dramatic irony for the audience, fully aware of his deceit. He claims that Mariana and Isabella are both mad, and are being used by some more powerful person, who is encouraging them to slander him. The Duke freely gives him permission to find out the truth and to punish them 'to [his] height of pleasure'. The Duke accuses both Friar Peter and Mariana of malicious intent and asks them whether they think that anything they could say could damage the proven reputation of a man such as Angelo. Escalus is invited to sit in judgement with Angelo, repeating the pattern set at the beginning of the play. The Duke orders that Friar Lodowick should be sent for. Reminding Angelo that once again he has full power to do 'as seems you best', the Duke leaves the stage.

Verse changes to prose as Escalus begins by questioning Lucio, who says that the friar's holy appearance does not match his morals and that he has insulted the Duke. Lucio is asked to remain and bear witness against him. Isabella is sent for, to be questioned again. Lucio, in language full of sexual innuendo, advises that Escalus should question her in private, and puns with sniggering relish on Escalus' intention to 'go darkly to work with her'.

Meanwhile, once more in disguise as Friar Lodowick, the Duke enters with Isabella and the Provost. Lucio says he recognises him, and Escalus asks him to keep quiet until he is called upon as a witness. Escalus asks the 'friar' if he encouraged the women to 'slander Lord Angelo'. Lying, he tells the 'friar' that the women have confessed (it seems an out-of-character assertion by the hitherto honest old counsellor). The 'friar' briefly says that this is not true, and Escalus asks him if he understands where he is. The 'friar' switches to verse in his reply. His words are confusing (or ironic) as he refers to respect for Escalus' 'great place' and honouring the devil in the same lines. He demands to know where the Duke is and, when told that the Duke's justice is represented by Escalus and Angelo, he tells the two women that they have no chance of justice: 'Come you to seek the lamb here of the fox?' He claims that the Duke is 'unjust' to make them appeal to the man that they are accusing. Lucio cannot wait to be asked to give his evidence and he interposes, 'This is the rascal'. Escalus orders that the 'friar' be taken to the rack to be tortured until he confesses his motives.

The 'friar' orders them not to be so hasty. In a speech full of dramatic irony, he says that that the Duke would not torture him, any more than he would torture himself. He asserts he is neither the Duke's subject, nor is he subject to the laws of Vienna, but his 'business in this state' has put him in the position of an observer, where he has 'seen corruption boil and bubble / Till it o'errun the stew'. This is an image from cookery, but it also refers to the 'stews' or brothels (see page 69). He claims that there are sufficient laws but they are not enforced, so they become mocked. Here, the 'friar' refers to the mock forfeits for unruly customers displayed in Jacobean barbers' shops. This is reminiscent of the images that he and Angelo each used earlier about laws that are not observed, in Act 1 Scene 3, lines 24–8 and Act 2 Scene 1, lines 1–4.

But the 'friar's' assertions simply anger Escalus, who indignantly accuses him of 'Slander to th'state'. Angelo, however, seems to require more proof and he calls upon Lucio to give his evidence. In his familiarly disrespectful manner, Lucio refers to the 'friar' as 'goodman Baldpate'. The 'friar' says that he recognises the sound of Lucio's voice, and as Lucio accuses him of speaking slanderously of the Duke, the 'friar' replies that the insults came from Lucio. Lucio claims to have pulled the 'friar's' nose for speaking wrongly of the Duke, but the 'friar' claims to 'love the Duke as I love myself'. Angelo is incensed and Escalus loses patience; he orders the 'friar' to be taken to prison with the two women ('giglets') and Friar Peter, 'the other confederate companion'. The Duke resists arrest and, during the physical struggle with Lucio which follows, Shakespeare hilariously prepares for Lucio's imminent downfall by having him direct a series of insults at the disguised Duke.

The dramatic trap is sprung as Lucio pulls off the 'friar's' hood to reveal the Duke. In the theatre it is a wonderfully comic moment as everyone on stage reacts to the 'discovery' of the Duke. Lucio is appalled as he realises he has dug a frightening pit for himself. Shakespeare reverts to verse as the Duke now assumes his rightful authority. He sardonically tells Lucio, 'Thou art the first knave that e'er mad'st a duke!', then orders the release of the two women and Friar Peter. There is another supremely comic moment as he orders Lucio not to sneak away (an in-built stage direction that indicates how Lucio is behaving), and warns him that he will be dealt with later. Lucio's groaning response, 'This may prove worse than hanging', usually evokes audience laughter in anticipation of what is to come. Escalus must have risen out of respect for the Duke's presence, but the Duke tells him to be re-seated, and he removes Angelo from his place of justice, demanding of him:

> Hast thou or word or wit or impudence
> That yet can do thee office? *(lines 356–7)*

Angelo does not prevaricate or ask what it is that the Duke knows. He compares the Duke to God who has observed all his behaviour. He asks that there be no delay; his confession should be followed by an immediate sentence and then death. The Duke calls Mariana to come forward, and Angelo admits that he was engaged to her. The Duke sends them both with Friar Peter to complete the marriage officially. Escalus is shocked by Angelo's 'dishonour'.

The Duke now turns to Isabella, telling her that he is still as attentive to her affairs as he was when disguised as a friar. Isabella asks for pardon that she should have unknowingly used her sovereign lord to deal with her concerns. The Duke formally forgives her, and asks her to be as generous ('free') in forgiving him for not preventing Claudio's death by exercising his rightful authority. The Duke tells her that it was the speed with which Claudio's execution was carried out that defeated his plans. He tells her to be comforted by the fact that Claudio is in a better place, and Isabella agrees. Just why the Duke, seemingly heartlessly, continues to keep Isabella in ignorance that her brother lives has been the focus of heated critical debate.

When Angelo and Mariana are brought back on stage, married, the Duke speaks of Angelo's 'salt imagination' (lecherous fantasies) and he asks Isabella to forgive him for Mariana's sake. However, as Angelo is guilty of the same crime as Claudio, and is also guilty in his intention to violate Isabella's chastity and the breaking of his promise to release Claudio after she had fulfilled her part of the bargain, he must suffer the same punishment:

> An Angelo for Claudio, death for death;
> Haste still pays haste, and leisure answers leisure;
> Like doth quit like, and measure still for measure. *(lines 402–4)*

The Duke declares that Angelo's guilt is clear and that he must die on the same block on which Claudio died, and with the same speed. Mariana pleads with the Duke but he replies that he has chosen to have Angelo marry Mariana in order to defend her honour. He also determines that, though legally Angelo's property falls to the Duke, the Duke will endow Mariana with it so that she will be a wealthy widow and will be able to buy a 'better husband'. Mariana pleads again that she craves 'no other, nor no better man'. The Duke refuses to alter his death sentence on Angelo, and Mariana kneels before him. The Duke says that she is wasting her time and turns to deal with Lucio. Mariana continues to entreat the Duke and begs Isabella to join her in supplication for Angelo's life, saying she will be indebted to her for life. The Duke intervenes to say that it is madness to ask Isabella; her brother's ghost would come back to prevent it. Mariana ignores the Duke's interjection and again implores Isabella to at least kneel with her and beg for mercy for Angelo silently; she does not have to speak. She excuses Angelo on the grounds that 'best men are moulded out of faults'. Again she begs Isabella to kneel. The Duke seems implacable: 'He dies for Claudio's death.'

There are conflicting considerations for Isabella. She is a novice nun and Christianity demands that she should be merciful, but she thinks that her brother is dead, executed by Angelo who has not kept his word. The audience's attention is fully on her as she experiences a moral crisis, and on stage there is often a long pause before Isabella does eventually kneel beside Mariana and speaks in Angelo's defence. Her reasons are that Angelo had led a virtuous life before he met her, and that Claudio did break the law. Shakespeare presumably intends there to be a pause to complete the line, 'For Angelo', as Isabella considers her argument in defence of Angelo. Her argument is complexly expressed: the sexual act he committed did not fulfil his intention to fornicate with Isabella, and mere intentions are not subject to the law.

His act did not o'ertake his bad intent,
And must be buried but as an intent
That perished by the way.   *(lines 444–6)*

Her reasoning seems odd as, for example, Claudio felt more strongly committed to Juliet than Angelo did to either Isabella or Mariana. Interestingly these are the last lines spoken by Isabella. Presumably Shakespeare intends that she will react to following events, but there are no stage directions to suggest what these reactions might be. Each actor playing the part must decide what seems to her to be appropriate behaviour for Isabella (see page 100).

The Duke dismisses the women's request for mercy and turns from them to consider why Claudio was beheaded at such an unusual time. He asks the Provost whether he had received a 'special warrant'. When the Provost says that it was by private message only, he dismisses him from his office ('Give up your keys'). The Provost apologises and says that at least he saved one other prisoner, Barnardine, who was also condemned by 'private order'. The Duke sends the Provost to fetch Barnardine.

Escalus grieves that someone who seemed 'so learned and so wise' as Angelo should have sinned, both in the heat of the moment and in more considered actions later. Angelo expresses his sorrow that he has caused so much grief:

And so deep sticks it in my penitent heart
That I crave death more willingly than mercy.   *(lines 468–9)*

The Provost returns with Barnardine, Claudio (who is hooded) and Juliet. The Duke addresses Barnardine, speaking of his 'stubborn soul' and telling him that he is 'condemned'. However, Shakespeare suggests that the Duke means condemned in the afterlife, because he tells Barnardine that he is forgiving him for his faults on earth and advises him to take this second chance to repent. He hands Barnardine over to Friar Peter for instruction.

The Duke asks, 'What muffled fellow's that?', and the Provost reveals that it is another prisoner who he saved from death, 'As like almost to Claudio as himself' and removes the hood from Claudio. It is another dramatic moment of 'unmasking' and the onstage audience usually reacts with amazement at this new 'discovery', a return from death to life. The Duke directly addresses Isabella, telling her that he pardons Claudio, but then goes on to make a brief proposal of marriage to her:

> Give me your hand, and say you will be mine,
> He is my brother too. *(lines 485–6)*

It is an intensely dramatic, an often totally unexpected moment. Just how does Isabella react? The history of the performance of the play is testament to the wildly varying responses that Isabella shows, from loving acceptance to horrified, frigid withdrawal (see page 100). The Duke's response to Isabella, 'But fitter time for that', gives few clues to help the actor, but offers endless possibilities to the director of the scene.

The Duke turns his attention to Angelo and pardons him too, warning him to love Mariana. He has now pardoned almost all those who have sinned during the course of the play, but he cannot forgive Lucio. Lucio claims it was all just a joke, and that it is the fashion to be satirical. He says he would rather be whipped for it than hanged. The Duke threateningly declares, 'Whipped first, sir, and hanged after.' He asks the Provost to issue a proclamation that if any woman has been wronged by him, Lucio will marry her. In Act 4, Lucio had admitted to the 'friar' that he had once been in court before the Duke, accused of fathering a child, and had denied it, even though it was true. Once he is married, Lucio is to be whipped and hung. Comically, Lucio seems much more shocked that the Duke intends to marry him to a prostitute than he is about his other punishments. The Duke pardons his offences and lets him off the sentence of death, but says he is definitely to marry. Lucio claims that 'Marrying a punk, my lord, is pressing to death, whipping, and hanging!' The Duke merely replies that it is what 'Slandering a prince' deserves.

The Duke's final speech seems intended to tie up all the loose ends of the play. He instructs Claudio to marry Juliet, wishes Mariana joy in her marriage to Angelo and assures Angelo that Mariana is virtuous. He thanks Escalus for his honest care, promising him further reward, and similarly thanks the Provost for his reticence and benevolence, promising him promotion. He asks Angelo to forgive the deception of the Provost in the substitution of Ragozine's head for Claudio's. Finally, the Duke again asks Isabella to marry him (again

Shakespeare gives her no response), and he leads the company from the stage. This final speech can be delivered and responded to in a manner that signifies that harmony is at last about to become the condition of Vienna and its personal relationships. But, especially over the past 100 years, stage performances have exploited its ambiguities and exposed its deceptive hopes for reconciliation. Isabella's response to the Duke's marriage proposal is open to the widest range of interpretations; Angelo's reaction to the prospect of lifelong marriage to Mariana is similarly ambiguously open. Many modern directors have taken advantage of the fact that a large number of Vienna's citizens are on stage to show that the city's corruption is still likely (or perhaps even more likely) to continue under the rule of the returned Duke, whose motivation for inflicting mental suffering on other characters for so long throughout the second half of the play remains perplexing and obscure. The final moments of many modern productions often reveal just why *Measure for Measure* has been characterised as a 'problem play' (see page 85).

Act 5: Critical review

In contrast to the many claustrophobic scenes of the play, this final scene is a very public event. The Duke takes his rightful place back in Vienna, witnessed by his people and welcomed by Angelo and Escalus. The atmosphere is heavy with dramatic irony. Just as when he was acting the role of the friar, the Duke is still acting a part because he is concealing his knowledge of what has occurred.

Isabella is tested and publicly shamed by the Duke who tells her to speak to Angelo, who will give her 'justice'. The Duke claims that he does not believe her story; he accuses her of being suborned by someone and plotting against the state. The 'friar' is mentioned but the Duke sends Isabella to prison. The dramatic tension is raised when Mariana comes forward, veiled, and in an ambiguous speech apparently defends Angelo from Isabella's accusation by asserting that he was with her, not Isabella. Again the 'friar' is blamed.

The Duke leaves the stage, and once more devolves his power to Angelo and Escalus. This time it is Escalus who dominates the trial, with Angelo an almost silent participant. In a thrillingly dramatic moment, the 'friar' is unmasked as the Duke. Angelo is appalled and contrite; he asks only for death. The Duke restores Mariana's honour by making Angelo marry her. Ensuring that the tension is maintained, the Duke apologises to Isabella for his failure to save Claudio. When Angelo and Mariana return to the stage as man and wife, the Duke insists on Angelo's death: 'An Angelo for Claudio, death for death', 'measure still for measure'. In one of the most dramatic moments in a tense act, Mariana begs Isabella to kneel with her to sue for Angelo's life.

The Duke seems to have achieved all his objectives. Angelo is aware of his humanity and shame, and Isabella has asked for mercy for Angelo. The Provost reveals that Barnardine and Claudio are alive, and there is only Lucio left to be punished. Though he is threatened with whipping and hanging, his final penalty is to restore the honour of the woman he had made pregnant by marrying her. The Duke again asks Isabella to marry him. She does not reply. This is an ending rich in possibilities for interpretation.

Contexts

This section identifies the contexts from which *Measure for Measure* emerged: the wide range of different influences that fostered the creativity of Shakespeare as he wrote the play. These contexts ensured that *Measure for Measure* is full of all kinds of reminders of everyday life, and the familiar knowledge, assumptions, beliefs and values of Jacobean England.

What did Shakespeare write?

Measure for Measure was first published in 1623 in the First Folio of Shakespeare's plays. Today, all editions of *Measure for Measure* are based on that 1623 version. This Guide follows the New Cambridge edition of the play (also used in the Cambridge School Shakespeare edition).

What did Shakespeare read?

Shakespeare's reading for *Measure for Measure* comes from several clearly identifiable sources. Some of these are other plays and stories, and European folk tales with such themes or titles as 'The Corrupt Magistrate', 'The Substituted Bride', and 'The Disguised Ruler'.

Most scholars agree that Shakespeare's major source for the thread of the plot that concerns Angelo and his bargain with Isabella was taken from the prose story of Epitia by an Italian writer, Cinthio, and included in his *Hecatommithi* (1565). The story was based on an incident which happened in Italy in 1547. Cinthio's tale concerns a young nobleman, Juriste, who is placed in charge of a city by the Emperor. In Cinthio's story the crime committed by the young man is rape (rather than the 'most mutual entertainment' of Claudio and Juliet). The sister of the condemned man, Epitia, goes to Juriste to plead for her brother's life, asking him to show mercy. Juriste makes the same offer to Epitia that Angelo makes to Isabella: an exchange of her virginity for her brother's life. She visits her brother in jail and he begs her to sacrifice herself for him and she agrees. Juriste promises to send Epitia's brother to her in the morning but then orders him to be beheaded even before he has slept with Epitia. He sends the body to her the next day. Epitia goes to the Emperor to demand justice. The

Emperor orders that Juriste must marry Epitia to restore her honour, but then he must be executed. Once they are married, Epitia pleads for Juriste's life and the Emperor finally agrees. In a later dramatic version of this story, Cinthio gives Juriste a sister, Angela, who also pleads for his life. Cinthio also adds a substituted head, keeping Epitia's brother alive.

A play (in two parts), *Promos and Cassandra*, written by the English playwright George Whetstone in 1578, uses a similar story. There is evidence in the structure of *Measure for Measure* to suggest that Shakespeare also knew Whetstone's play, in particular the use of a comic sub-plot involving lower-class characters.

As is frequently the case in the study of Shakespeare's sources, the interest lies in what he changes. There is a major alteration in the character of Isabella. In each of the other stories she submits, and in none of the source stories is she a nun. The figure of Lucio is also a major addition found in none of the source stories, bridging the main plot and the sub-plot. He adds a humorous perspective to the main plot and deflates the tendency towards pomposity in some of the other major characters.

Critics also consider that Shakespeare used sections of King James' own work on the practice of government, *Basilicon Doron* ('The King's Gift'). This was a work that James had written for his son to give him advice on manners, morals and the ways of kingship. James refers to the Bible throughout, and in relation to the law and to justice, he reminds his son that Christ died to redeem the sins of humanity. You will find other ways in which King James is often considered to be one of Shakespeare's inspirations for the play on pages 65–66 below.

Certain speeches and plot devices also seem to have their roots in Shakespeare's reading. For example the 'friar's' advice to Claudio in Act 3 Scene 1 has similarities with 'The Art of Dying' (*Ars Moriendi*), which instructed Man how to prepare to meet Death and how to avoid the temptation of sin. The 'bed-trick' had a long history in folk tales and was a fairly common dramatic device in Renaissance plays. Similarly the 'disguised ruler' was a relatively common device in Renaissance drama in which monarchs assumed a disguise to wander freely among their subjects. Shakespeare would have known many such plays or stories, but he was possibly much influenced by a work by George Whetstone, *A Mirrour for Magistrates of Cities* (1584). In this prose work concerning law and justice, Whetstone condemns what he describes as the growth of crime and vice in London. He says that the laws are unobserved, merely 'written threatninges', perhaps giving rise to Shakespeare's images of the unused birch and the ignored scarecrow in *Measure for Measure*. The convention of the stage requires that a disguise, however limited in terms of costume, must be completely impenetrable to the other characters until it is removed. As Jacobeans were so familiar with the tradition, they would have had no difficulty in accepting – and enjoying – the impenetrability of the Duke's disguise.

What was Shakespeare's England like?

Shakespeare sets *Measure for Measure* in Vienna, but his Vienna has clear parallels with Jacobean England, particularly London. It is rooted firmly in an urban environment that would have been recognisable to Shakespeare's contemporary audience in many ways. For example, discipline in families tended to be quite strict, so that fathers who did not beat their children with a birch were held to be 'fond' or foolish. Legal punishments were correspondingly harsh, with many crimes punishable by death. When the Duke as friar is suspected of treason, he is threatened with being sent to the rack. Humiliation was an everyday punishment and Claudio is being made an example to others, being shamed by being publicly paraded through the streets by special commission from Angelo. In Act 5, Lucio makes a reference to the fact that even animals were punished harshly; dogs could be hung for worrying sheep, 'Show your sheep-biting face, and be hanged an hour!'

All the crimes described by Pompey in the prison would have been acknowledged as common offences. In Act 4 Scene 3, lines 1–16, Pompey comments on his fellow inmates. In 1604 a 'statute of stabbing' had been passed in an attempt by the authorities to cut down the number of street-brawls by 'roaring boys' in London. Pompey describes a number of such wild young men: 'Master Starvelackey . . . young Dropheir . . . Master Forthright . . . and wild Halfcan', all in prison for fighting. He also speaks of 'Master Rash' being in prison for devious commercial practice, dealing in commodities; that is, the practice of making part of a loan in kind, and greatly overvaluing the commodity to avoid the 10 per cent legal limit on the rate of interest.

Pompey describes all the prisoners he mentions as frequenters of brothels, adding to the atmosphere of the corrupt underworld of

Vienna. Pompey's final line in this speech, 'and are now "for the Lord's sake"', refers to the fact that prisoners had to pay for everything in prison: food, bedding, even their release. These prisoners are penniless and have to beg from the windows, 'for the Lord's sake' being a common cry of beggars. In Act 5 the Duke refers to the mock punishments for bad behaviour in a barber's shop. These punishments were frequently gory, and concerned other aspects of a barber's work, those of tooth-drawer, blood-letter and surgeon.

Lucio mentions the prospect of war in Act 1 Scene 2, lines 1–3: 'If the Duke, with the other dukes, come not to composition with the King of Hungary, why then all the dukes fall upon the King.' The reference to Hungary is significant because there had been a long-running war in Europe, involving Hungary, and England was possibly involved in negotiations with her allies for soldiers to fight in the war. The possibility of war would have been a tempting prospect for professional soldiers, as the gentlemen talking to Lucio seem to be.

Elbow is paid to carry out the office of constable. This was becoming a common practice, as citizens who were eligible to take a term of duty as constable for their ward or parish found themselves too busy to undertake the office. Shakespeare tended to make fun of constables, suggesting that they tried to use language that was above their station. However, he usually presents them as well-intentioned and 'ironically' successful.

Angelo is described as 'precise', a word frequently applied to Puritans. Puritan objections to the theatre seem to have led Shakespeare to ridicule Puritans in other plays, for example in *Twelfth Night* in the character of Malvolio. Though much of England was relatively tolerant, the City of London was increasingly controlled by Puritan Lord Mayors and Aldermen. They tended to see prostitution as a threat to good public order, and some even advocated the death penalty for prostitutes, but not for their clients (evidence of the commonplace double standard towards women, as demonstrated by the Duke when he tells Juliet that her sin is 'of heavier kind' than Claudio's). The Puritan authorities in London also hated the theatre because they felt that it offered opportunities for seditious material to be promulgated. Puritans disapproved of anything that interfered with work, and there is evidence that they particularly objected to apprentices attending the theatre.

All the above examples show how *Measure for Measure* reflects aspects of Shakespeare's times. What now follows are other significant ways in which the play reveals its context: the structure, culture and beliefs of Jacobean England.

James I

Queen Elizabeth had died in 1603 and James VI of Scotland inherited the throne. Critics have detected certain aspects of his personality in the play, particularly in the character of the Duke. For example, James was a suspicious man and he was known to dislike noisy crowds. The Duke also says that he dislikes crowds: 'I do not relish well / Their loud applause and aves vehement'. This may be an oblique reference to James' private visit to see the preparations and street decorations for his coronation. The general public heard about the visit and many rushed to see him. James had to take refuge in the Exchange and have the doors locked. Angelo's speech concerning the effects of Isabella's impending visit may also be a reference to James' dislike of crowds:

> even so
> The general subject to a well-wished king
> Quit their own part and in obsequious fondness
> Crowd to his presence, where their untaught love
> Must needs appear offence.   *(Act 2 Scene 4, lines 26–30)*

James felt that he had possibly been too lax in his rule in Scotland but he was eager to be considered a merciful ruler. At Winchester he reprieved a number of condemned men at the very last moment before they were to be put to death, just as the Duke does with Claudio, Angelo, Barnardine and Lucio.

Though it would be unwise to try to interpret *Measure for Measure* as written merely as a compliment to James, Shakespeare's company had been quickly appointed on James' succession as his acting company, the King's Men. The public records state that *Mesur for Mesur* by Shaxberd (Shakespeare – spelling of English had not yet been standardised) was performed at court in December 1604. From the point of view of the King's Men it would have been politic to include some issues that would interest their new patron, just as the subject matter for any play due to be performed at court would have been influenced by the tastes of the sovereign.

James was a scholarly man and wrote several books on various topics, including demonology and tobacco. Though the position and duties of a king were topics of current interest and debate, in *Measure for Measure* there is another possible reference to James' work *Basilicon Doron* (see page 62) in the Duke's soliloquy concerning the role of the sovereign:

> He who the sword of heaven will bear
> Should be as holy, as severe:
> Pattern in himself to know,
> Grace to stand, and virtue go   *(Act 3 Scene 2, lines 223–6)*

James believed very strongly that his position as king made him God's representative on earth and he expresses very forcefully in *Basilicon Doron* that his son should, like himself, stand as a 'pattern' of self-knowledge and virtue for his subjects. He believed that his authority was based upon Divine Right (a principle that was also held by Charles I and which led to the English Revolution and Charles' execution). In several works written in the sixteenth and seventeenth centuries, scholars had explored the idea of the 'Great Chain of Being' with the king at the top, legitimising the differences between the rich and the poor, the power-holders and the powerless, as coming from God. James was also known to be very sensitive about his personal image and to resent slander deeply. The severe punishment meted out to Lucio for 'Slandering a prince' would almost certainly have met with his approval.

The Bible

The title of the play appears to be derived from the Gospel of St Matthew, Chapter 7, verse 2: 'with what measure ye mete, it shall be measured to you again'. One of the themes of the play is the conflict between the Old Testament judgement of 'life for life, eye for eye, tooth for tooth', and the New Testament doctrine of forgiveness. Though the Duke's words in condemning Angelo echo the Old Testament phrasing, 'An Angelo for Claudio, death for death', (Act 5 Scene 1, line 402), at the end of the play he bestows Christian mercy.

In Act 1, when the Duke is telling Angelo that he is to be his deputy, he tells him that he must not hide his light under a bushel, and that his talents have not been given to him to be left unused (Scene 1, lines 29–35). Each of these images refers to parables told by Christ according to the Gospel of St Matthew.

Though *Measure for Measure* should not necessarily be read as a Christian allegory, it is full of references to the Bible that would have been extremely familiar to Shakespeare's audiences, particularly the 'Sermon on the Mount' recorded in Matthew 5–7 and Luke 6, and phrases from the Bible that had become common expressions. The 'Sermon on the Mount' was a common topic for readings and lessons in English churches and was a compulsory annual subject for a sermon based on the version in St Luke's Gospel. Shakespeare would have been very familiar with the doctrine of Christian forgiveness as expressed in the 'Sermon on the Mount' and could have been certain that his audience was too. The injunctions to practise mercy in order to receive it, and not to judge others as you hope not to be judged yourself, were ideas that were also linked to the contemporary debate on the proper exercise of power and justice.

The clearest allusions to the teachings of the New Testament are in the references to mercy Isabella makes in her impassioned pleas to Angelo in Act 2 Scene 2, culminating in:

> How would you be
> If he, which is the top of judgement, should
> But judge you as you are? Oh, think on that,
> And mercy then will breathe within your lips
> Like man new made.   *(lines 77–81)*

Isabella's final entreaty in Act 5 for Angelo to be forgiven appears as irrational as Christ's instruction to love one's enemies, and Shakespeare's audience would have recognised the parallel.

Marriage

One of the hotly debated points in *Measure for Measure* is the status of the 'marriage' of Claudio and Juliet, and there has been a great deal of debate among Shakespearean critics about the precise kinds of marriage vows that are made in *Measure for Measure*. There is a general consensus that Angelo's contract to Mariana is in law at least as binding as Claudio's to Juliet and that Shakespeare intends an equivalence of situation.

Claudio's contract of marriage to Juliet is usually taken to be *sponsalia per verba de praesenti*, that is a solemn and binding agreement made between two people, possibly, but not always, in front of witnesses, that was a legal contract, even though it had not been formally ratified by the calling of banns and a church ceremony:

> Upon a true contract
> I got possession of Julietta's bed –
> You know the lady, she is fast my wife,
> Save that we do the denunciation lack
> Of outward order.   *(Act 1 Scene 2, lines 126–30)*

Many couples lived all their lives as man and wife with no further ceremony in church, though Claudio makes it clear that once Juliet's friends had agreed to the marriage, and agreed therefore to release Juliet's dowry, they would have asked for the blessing of the Church.

The Duke describes Mariana's case as being similar: 'She should this Angelo have married – was affianced to her oath, and the nuptial appointed; between which time of the contract, and limit of the solemnity, her brother Frederick was wrecked at sea, having in that perished vessel the dowry of his sister' (Act 3 Scene 1, lines 204–8). This is a contract to marry ('solemnity') in the future, *sponsalia per verba de futuro*, but was considered equally binding, though subject to circumstances. Angelo chose to consider that the failure of the financial arrangements released him from the contract. The sexual consummation of their agreement to marry, planned by the Duke, would confirm the legal status of their marriage.

Marriage between people from the higher orders of Renaissance society were more likely to be constrained by considerations of property; and because it involved property and inheritance, the legality of marriage was paramount. Further down the social scale, English common law recognised verbal contracts of marriage which had not been ratified by the Church. Shakespeare and his wife had their first child only six months after the church celebration of their marriage.

Church authorities felt very strongly that the ceremony and sacrament of marriage should precede consummation, and pressed for the punishment of those who slept together without the blessing of the Church. Claudio is condemned for fornication, but Shakespeare makes it clear to the audience that his attitude to Juliet is very different from Lucio's to Kate Keepdown. Lucio promised marriage to Kate, according to Mistress Overdone, and then backed out when he had made her pregnant. When Shakespeare wrote *Measure for Measure* attitudes to marriage were changing, just as some social historians would claim they are changing at present.

Sexuality

In Act 5 the Duke refers to the 'stews', or brothels in Vienna. The area on Bankside where the Globe was situated was where many of the 'stews', bathhouses and taverns were located, just out of the jurisdiction of the Puritan authorities. No doubt Shakespeare would have passed them daily when working at the Globe.

The appropriateness of the control of sexuality was part of a contemporary debate during Shakespeare's time, and he powerfully dramatises the conflict between current points of view. St Augustine had argued that brothels were a necessary release for lust: 'Suppress prostitution and capricious lusts will overthrow society.' St Thomas Aquinas had put forward a similar justification for prostitution: 'Prostitution in the towns is like the cesspool in the palace: take away the cesspool and the palace will become an unclean and evil-smelling place.' These kinds of arguments were used particularly by those in high places who received part of their income from property leased to brothels, like the 'wise burgher' who 'put in for them' in Act 1 of *Measure for Measure*, or like the Bishop of Winchester in Shakespeare's time, who owned property on Bankside leased for brothels. Certain Puritan authorities wanted all brothels closed.

Pompey puts forward the view that sexuality is a natural force, only to be controlled by physical mutilation: 'to geld and splay'. Lucio also tells the Duke it is 'impossible to extirp it quite, friar, till eating and drinking be put down', suggesting that sex is as necessary as food and drink. These views are supported to some extent by the more moderate Provost, 'All sects, all ages smack of this vice', and he describes Claudio as 'a young man / More fit to do another such offence / Than die for this'. The question whether the State had the legitimate right to control sexuality continued to be hotly debated for another 45 years after the first performance of *Measure for Measure*, culminating in draconian laws like Angelo's being passed by the Commonwealth in 1650, after the execution of Charles I. Incest and adultery were punishable by death, fornicators were to be imprisoned, and brothel-keepers could be whipped, pilloried, branded and jailed for up to three years. If they were caught offending a second time, the punishment was death.

In *Measure for Measure* Shakespeare brings the debate between 'restraint' and 'liberty' into sharp dramatic focus. Is Angelo and Isabella's extreme 'restraint' more damaging than Claudio's 'too much liberty'? Is Pompey ('a poor fellow that would live') worse than Angelo?

Sexually transmitted diseases were a major problem in England by 1604, particularly in London. The familiarity with which Lucio and the two Gentlemen joke about their possible symptoms, and the ironically vivid language they use, with its own specialised vocabulary, shows how common these diseases had become. The images of disease, decay and corruption associated with unrestrained sexuality stand in sharp contrast to Lucio's description of Juliet's pregnancy in Act 1 Scene 4, with its lyrical poetic qualities and suggestion of a natural, fruitful harvest.

There are many sexual euphemisms that may escape a modern audience, such as 'a game of tick-tack', which was a popular game where scoring was by means of placing pegs in holes. Shakespeare's contemporary audience would also have appreciated the macabre bawdy jokes relating to sexually transmitted diseases. In Act 1 Scene 2, the first Gentleman refers to the continuing conflict with France as he argues for his preference for 'English kersey' over 'French velvet', making a conventional reference to syphilis as the French disease. Lucio and the Gentlemen comment on each other's physical symptoms of venereal disease, or more likely the effects of the 'cures'. One common so-called remedy for syphilis was mercury and this caused the sufferer's hair to fall out, making him bald, or 'pilled'. The references to a 'French crown' and 'hollow bones' and 'sciatica' also referred to the effects of sexually transmitted diseases and would have been commonplace terms in 1604.

In Act 1 Scene 2, Mistress Overdone refers to her failing trade and bemoans her lack of customers: 'what with the war, what with the sweat, what with the gallows, and what with poverty, I am custom-shrunk' (lines 68–9). Commentators on *Measure for Measure* have identified various topical issues relevant to 1603–4 here that would have been recognised by the audience. There was a continuing war with Spain and soldiers were notorious for their use of prostitutes.

The outbreak of the plague ('the sweat') that year had been especially severe. Because there had been quite a high incidence of social unrest there had been an unusually large number of trials and executions for treason, and in that time of extremely high inflation there was a great deal of poverty.

Later in the same scene (line 80), Pompey tells Mistress Overdone of the 'proclamation, 'All houses in the suburbs of Vienna must be plucked down.' In 1603 a proclamation had been issued that certain London houses should be 'plucked down' in order to prevent the continued spread of a particularly virulent outbreak of the plague. Among those houses that were pulled down were various brothels. Even the rambling story told by Pompey when he is arrested with Froth referred to a popular dish served in brothels: 'stewed prunes', which also had bawdy connotations.

The position of women

The social position of women at the time is reflected in the play. All the women in *Measure for Measure* are in socially ambivalent positions as none of them is either married or apparently under the control of a father. None of them has any power over her own life. Isabella is the only woman to play a major part in the play in terms of the number of lines that she speaks. She is withdrawing from society, seeking a more 'strict restraint' than that imposed even by the standards of the Poor Clares. Juliet is a victim of 'too much liberty' whilst waiting for her relations to agree to her marriage and release her dowry. The man who promised to marry Mariana abandoned her when her dowry was lost, with her brother, in an accident at sea; 'her promisèd proportions / Came short of composition', and he was also able, apparently unchallenged, to claim that her 'reputation was disvalued / In levity'. Mistress Overdone and Kate Keepdown appear to make their living by trading in sex, Mistress Overdone by running a brothel and then a bathhouse (bathhouses and hot-houses were also likely to be brothels). Lucio refers to Kate Keepdown as a 'rotten medlar' or prostitute, though apparently she believed him when he promised her marriage.

Convents and monasteries

The significance of Isabella's role as a nun and the Duke's disguise as a friar is the subject of much critical debate, as there would have been very few – if any – monks or nuns in London in 1604. By the end of

1539 most of the religious houses had been closed and their land sold off by Henry VIII for various reasons. Henry's public justification was that they were corrupt and that they gave their supreme allegiance to Rome rather than to the king. Some critics suggest that Shakespeare's intention is to show the devoutness of the Duke and to bring a religious ethos more centrally into the themes of the play. These critics sometimes go so far as to suggest that Shakespeare had Catholic sympathies.

Other critics say that nuns and friars would be either figures of fun or of contempt during this period, citing evidence from earlier writers such as Chaucer who satirised the behaviour of some monks and nuns. However, there is no evidence in *Measure for Measure* that Shakespeare intended to suggest that Isabella is regarded with contempt or ridicule as a novice nun, and the Duke as friar seems to be respected by all the other characters in the play, except for Lucio.

Money

During Shakespeare's time there was no equivalent of paper money, though there were written promissory notes. All 'real' money was in coins and the value of the coin was absolutely equivalent to its weight in gold or silver. In a time of raging inflation there was consequent doubt about the genuineness of money and great fear of forgery. *Measure for Measure* has many references to the theme of testing and forgery (coining). Angelo uses images taken from forgery; for example, he asks that 'there be some more test made of my metal / Before so noble and so great a figure / Be stamped upon it' (Act 1 Scene 1, lines 48–50). This is a pun on his own name because gold coins were called angels or nobles. There is also a pun on 'metal' and mettle, or spirit. In Act 2 Scene 4, in his debate with Isabella, Angelo speaks of fornicators as those who 'coin heaven's image / In stamps that are forbid' (lines 44–5).

'Assaying' (testing) gold or silver was performed by rubbing it with a piece of quartz (a 'touchstone'). The colour of the mark made showed the quality of the metal. Claudio asks Lucio to find his sister and send her to 'assay' Angelo, and the Duke tells Claudio that Angelo was only attempting to 'assay' the virtue of his sister. There is a sense in which *Measure for Measure* is about the way that the Duke puts Angelo in place as his deputy to test or 'assay' his worth.

Language

In *Shakespeare's Language*, Frank Kermode comments that in *Measure for Measure* the 'poetry, often as fine as any in the canon, is all in the tragedy'. He shows less admiration for the language in the second half of the play. Many critics have commented on the change in the expressiveness of the language and imagery which occurs after Act 3 Scene 1, line 152, but other critics argue that Shakespeare seems to have had different priorities and objectives in the latter part of *Measure for Measure*. Having established the debates and the characters, there then remains the resolution to be worked out by the Duke. In performance, the second half of the play is often easier for a first-time spectator to follow than the intellectual debate of the first half.

Throughout the play Shakespeare uses a wide variety of language registers, from the formality of the conversations between the Duke and Escalus to the colloquial banter between Lucio and his drinking companions; from the intellectually demanding discussion between Angelo and Isabella with its sexual subtext to the convoluted excuses of Pompey and muddle-headedness of Elbow. Shakespeare gives each of the major characters a distinctive voice. The pervasive wordplay reflects the way that Shakespeare plays with language to explore multi-level meanings. It constantly reminds the audience of the duplicity of language.

But for all such distinctive (and sometimes daunting) qualities of the language of *Measure for Measure*, Shakespeare employs in the play the same language techniques he used throughout his entire playwriting career in order to intensify dramatic effect, create mood and character, and so produce memorable theatre. Those techniques are found alike in the play's prose and verse. What follows is an analysis of some of those language techniques. As you read the play, always keep in mind that Shakespeare wrote for the stage, and that actors will therefore employ a wide variety of both verbal and non-verbal methods to exploit the dramatic possibilities of the language. They will use the full range of their voices and accompany the words with appropriate expressions, gestures and actions.

Imagery

Measure for Measure abounds in imagery, especially in the first half of the play. It is particularly evident in the various debates that recur. Imagery (sometimes called 'figures' or 'figurative language') is formed of vivid words and phrases that help create the atmosphere of the play as they conjure up emotionally-charged mental pictures and associations in the imagination. Shakespeare seems to have thought in images, and the whole play richly demonstrates his unflagging and varied use of verbal illustration, particularly in his use of sexual images. For example, when Angelo speaks of his desire for Isabella, his image is of someone receiving the sacrament (the bread and wine of Christian communion) but still committing sin in his thoughts. The sacrament should follow confession and repentance, but Angelo is aware that he cannot repent the lustful thoughts he has about Isabella:

> Heaven in my mouth
> As if I did but only chew his name,
> And in my heart the strong and swelling evil
> Of my conception.   *(Act 2 Scene 4, lines 4–7)*

Here he evokes not only his passion for Isabella, but brings to mind for the audience the sacrilege that he contemplates of forcing a nun to have sex with him, and the physical manifestations of desire that he is experiencing. There is also the implication of the possible consequences of their sexual relations in his pun on 'conception'.

Early critics, such as John Dryden and Doctor Johnson, were critical of Shakespeare's fondness for imagery. They felt that many images obscured meaning and detracted attention from the subjects they represented. Over the past 200 years, however, critics, poets and audiences have increasingly valued Shakespeare's imagery. They recognise how he uses it to give pleasure as it stirs the audience's imagination, deepens the dramatic impact of particular moments or moods, provides insight into character, and intensifies meaning and emotional force. Images carry powerful significance far deeper than their surface meanings, and some critics have detected dominant or repeated images ('iterative imagery') running through the play, notably those of sex, desire and coinage.

As the Contexts section of this Guide shows, Shakespeare's Elizabethan and Jacobean world provides much of the play's imagery.

For example, page 7 notes many images of sexually transmitted diseases as Lucio and his friends joke about them in Act 1 Scene 2. Elsewhere, euphemisms for the sexual act provide a rich source of images, possibly more than in any other of Shakespeare's plays: 'Groping for trouts in a peculiar river', 'our most mutual entertainment', 'a game of tick-tack', 'his full tilth and husbandry', 'your most offenceful act', 'saucy sweetness', 'sweet uncleanness', 'yielding up your body to my will', 'the momentary trick', 'the rebellion of a codpiece', 'filling a bottle with a tundish', 'Gift of my chaste body / To his concupiscible intemperate lust'. There are also many words which had a bawdy connotation recognisable to Shakespeare's contemporaries, though possibly not for a modern audience, for example in Act 2 Scene 1 during Pompey's long account of what happened to Elbow's wife: 'stewed prunes', 'dish', 'pin', 'point', 'two', and 'stones'.

Images of coining also recur. For example, an image that would have been familiar to Jacobeans in a time of high inflation, when forgery was rife, occurs when Angelo asks:

> Let there be some more test made of my metal
> Before so noble and so great a figure
> Be stamped upon it.   *(Act 1 Scene 1, lines 48–50)*

The coining image is ironic. Angelo is tested and proved to be false. Shakespeare's contemporary audience would also have recognised that an 'angel' (Angelo) and a 'noble' were coins. Angelo uses another image taken from coining and forgery when he rails against those who 'coin heaven's image / In stamps that are forbid' (Act 2 Scene 4 lines, 44–5), suggesting that children who are born outside marriage are forgeries.

Shakespeare's imagery uses metaphor, simile or personification. All are comparisons that in effect substitute one thing (the image) for another (the thing described). *Measure for Measure* is particularly rich in complex metaphors.

- A *simile* compares one thing to another using 'like' or 'as', for example when the Duke speaks of the unenforced laws: 'like an o'er-grown lion in a cave / That goes not out to prey' (Act 1 Scene 3, lines 23–4). In another telling simile he describes the effects of

Angelo's rejection of Mariana. 'His unjust unkindness' has increased her love for him and 'like an impediment in the current [of a river] made it more violent and unruly' (Act 3 Scene 1, lines 228–9). Earlier in this scene, Claudio has told Isabella in a complex image that if he must die, 'I will encounter darkness as a bride / And hug it in mine arms' (lines 83–4).

- A *metaphor* is also a comparison, suggesting that two dissimilar things are actually the same. Angelo reflects:

> Having waste ground enough
> Shall we desire to raze the sanctuary
> And pitch our evils there?   (*Act 2 Scene 2, lines 174–6*)

Here the comparison is between 'waste ground' or prostitutes, and Angelo's intention to 'raze' or destroy a holy place (to take Isabella's virginity) and pitch the tent of his evil actions in its place ('pitch' also has the connotation of blackness).

The Duke claims that while he was disguised as a friar, he saw 'corruption boil and bubble / Till it o'errun the stew' (Act 5 Scene 1, lines 314–15). This homely image is taken from cookery, but it also suggests the way that fornication is spreading from the 'stews' or brothels to corrupt society. Lucio's particularly effective and lyrical image describing Juliet's pregnancy conveys a sense of the natural and positive qualities associated with harvest and plenty (see page 11).

- *Personification* turns all kinds of abstractions into persons, giving them human feelings or attributes. For example, in Act 1 Scene 3 the Duke tells Friar Thomas that 'Liberty plucks Justice by the nose' (line 30), emphasising the mockery of the law. In Act 1 Scene 2, Claudio describes 'surfeit' (excess) as 'the father of much fast [restraint]', and in Act 1 Scene 4, Lucio compares himself to a 'lapwing' because these birds pretend to be distressed some distance from the nest to deceive predators. Lucio admits that his habit is to deceive women 'to jest / Tongue far from heart' (lines 32–3).

Antithesis

Antithesis is the opposition of words or phrases against each other, as when the Duke confers his power on Angelo, 'Mortality and mercy in

Vienna / Live in thy tongue and heart' (Act 1 Scene 1, lines 44–5), and a little later reminds him that he may 'enforce or qualify the laws' (line 65). This setting of word against word ('Mortality' stands in contrast to 'mercy', and 'enforce' opposes 'qualify') is one of Shakespeare's favourite language devices. He uses it extensively in all his plays. Why? Because antithesis powerfully expresses conflict through its use of opposites, and conflict is the essence of all drama. Shakespeare's dramatic style is characterised by his concern for comparison and contrast, opposition and juxtaposition: he sets character against character, scene against scene, emotional tone against emotional tone.

In *Measure for Measure*, conflict occurs in many forms: Angelo is forced into public life when the Duke chooses to retire to his disguised role as friar; Isabella is forced into public life from her noviciate. One character or action is set against another: Angelo against the Duke; Angelo against Isabella; Angelo and Mariana's betrothal against that of Claudio and Juliet; Angelo's fornication against Claudio's. The Duke's advice to Claudio, 'Be absolute for death', is opposed by Claudio's speech, 'Ay, but to die'.

Antithesis intensifies the sense of conflict, and is embodied in the structure of the play, in the setting of scene against scene. For instance, with a sense of opposing qualities in his characters, Shakespeare balances the scenes where Claudio speaks of his acceptance of guilt with the mock trial of Pompey, who refuses to acknowledge culpability: 'If your worship will take order for the drabs and the knaves, you need not to fear the bawds' (Act 2 Scene 1, lines 200–2).

Such conflict is also embodied in the language of the play, as Shakespeare sets word against word, phrase against phrase. Angelo wonders 'The tempter or the tempted, who sins most, ha?' (Act 2 Scene 2, line 168). Isabella weighs her chastity against her brother's life: 'Then Isabel live chaste, and brother die' (Act 2, Scene 4, line 185). Claudio twice balances his wish for life with his readiness for death: 'I have hope to live, and am prepared to die' (Act 3 Scene 1, line 4); 'To sue to live, I find I seek to die, / And seeking death find life' (Act 3 Scene 1, lines 42–3).

One sequence of antitheses centres on Angelo. Again and again he is measured against Claudio. Escalus asks him,

> Whether you had not sometime in your life
> Erred in this point which now you censure him,
> And pulled the law upon you.　　　*(Act 2 Scene 1, lines 14–16)*

Angelo responds with unconscious irony:

> When I that censure him do so offend,
> Let mine own judgement pattern out my death
> And nothing come in partial.　　　*(Act 2 Scene 1, lines 29–31)*

This pattern of judging Angelo against Claudio recurs throughout the play. It is repeated by Isabella thee times in Act 2 Scene 2: in lines 65–7, 77–9 and 140–3. The Duke reiterates the antithesis in Act 4 Scene 2, lines 70–3 and Act 5 Scene 1, lines 111–12. This culminates in the final judgement given by the Duke:

> An Angelo for Claudio, death for death;
> Haste still pays haste, and leisure answers leisure;
> Like doth quit like, and measure still for measure.
> *(Act 5 Scene 1, lines 402–4)*

Repetition

Different forms of language repetition run through the play, contributing to its atmosphere, creation of character and dramatic impact. Shakespeare's skill in using repetition to heighten theatrical effect and deepen emotional and imaginative significance is most evident in particular speeches. Repeated words, phrases, rhythms and sounds add intensity to the moment or episode. A striking example is the notion of 'seeming', which gains emphasis as the various forms of the word are repeated through the play. Speaking of Angelo, the Duke says 'Hence shall we see, / If power change purpose, what our seemers be' (Act 1 Scene 3, lines 54–5). When faced with Angelo's monstrous bargain, Isabella cries, 'Seeming, seeming' (Act 2 Scene 4, line 151). The Duke tells Isabella of Angelo's conduct towards Mariana, describing him as 'this well-seeming Angelo'. Isabella's plea to the Duke is 'To make the truth appear where it seems hid, / And hide the false seems true' (Act 5 Scene 1, lines 66–7).

The nature of justice is a major theme of the play, and repetition of the word when Isabella demands 'justice, justice, justice, justice' contributes power to the final scene and draws the audience's attention to the climax of the debate. The word 'tomorrow' is also stressed throughout the play to add to the atmosphere of intensity and to give a sense of the necessity for speed of action. Other words that recur frequently in *Measure for Measure* include 'mercy', 'liberty', 'authority', 'blood' and 'grace'. The effect of the repetition varies with each use of the word. For example, 'sense' is a word repeated throughout the play, but Shakespeare draws attention to the different meanings of the word by Angelo's use of 'sense' in consecutive lines, setting 'good reason' against 'sexual desire':

> She speaks, and 'tis such sense
> That my sense breeds with it.   *(Act 2 Scene 2, lines 146–7)*

The repeated rhythms of verse are discussed below, but the play's prose also contains similar qualities of rhythmical and phrase repetition, as, for example, in Pompey's defence in Act 2 Scene 1, where his repetition of 'as I say', 'as I said' conveys the impression of a gossipy narrative. Subtle rhythmical and lexical repetitions are found in the prose dialogue between the Duke and Isabella in Act 3: 'The hand that hath made you fair hath made you good: the goodness that is cheap in beauty makes beauty brief in goodness; but grace, being the soul of your complexion, shall keep the body of it ever fair' (Scene 1, lines 176–9).

Lists

One of Shakespeare's favourite language methods is to accumulate words or phrases rather like a list. He had learned the technique as a schoolboy in Stratford-upon-Avon, and his skill in knowing how to use lists dramatically is evident in *Measure for Measure*. He intensifies and varies description, atmosphere and argument as he 'piles up' item on item, incident on incident. Such 'lists' may be brief, as in the Duke's description of Angelo's public image, 'Lord Angelo is precise, / Stands at a guard with envy, scarce confesses / That his blood flows, or that his appetite / Is more to bread than stone' (Act 1 Scene 3, lines 51–4), in Isabella's catalogue of symbols of great authority, 'the king's crown, nor the deputed sword, / The marshal's truncheon, nor the judge's robe' (Act 2 Scene 2, lines 61–2), or in her anguished response to the news that Claudio has been executed, 'Unhappy Claudio, wretched

Isabel, / Injurious world, most damnèd Angelo!' (Act 4 Scene 3, lines 113–14).

Other speeches contain much longer lists. The most notable example is the Duke's speech in Act 3 Scene 1, lines 5–41, 'Be absolute for death', where his unrelenting list of the disadvantages of life temporarily convinces Claudio. In opposition to this speech, when Claudio is faced with the immediate fact of his death, he responds with his own list of pains to be suffered in the afterlife. In a quite different emotional tone, Pompey's detailed listing of the prisoners (Act 4 Scene 3, lines 3–16) offers the actor many comic opportunities (as well as giving the audience an insight into the varied nature of London's lowlife, see page 63). In Act 5 Isabella lists the ways in which Angelo had seemed virtuous, matching this list with another of the ways in which he is villainous (lines 52–7).

The lists in the play provide valuable opportunities for actors to vary their delivery. In speaking, an actor usually seeks to give each 'item' a distinctiveness in emphasis and emotional tone, and sometimes an accompanying action and expression. In addition, the accumulating effect of lists can add to the force of argument, enrich atmosphere, amplify meaning and provide extra dimensions of character.

Verse and prose

Much of *Measure for Measure* is in prose. How did Shakespeare decide whether to write in verse or prose? One answer is that he followed theatrical convention. Comic and low-status characters traditionally used prose. High-status characters spoke verse. 'Comic' scenes were written in prose (as were letters and 'mad' scenes), but audiences expected verse in 'serious' scenes: the poetic style was thought to be particularly suitable for lovers and for moments of high dramatic or emotional intensity. So prose was felt appropriate to comedy, verse to tragedy and history plays.

But Shakespeare used his judgement about which conventions or principles he should follow, and the play shows that he increasingly broke the 'rules'. In earlier comedies (*The Comedy of Errors*, *The Two Gentlemen of Verona*, *A Midsummer Night's Dream*), his upper-class characters, although comic, usually speak in verse. But in *Measure for Measure* Shakespeare switches often from prose to verse, for example in the conversation between Lucio and Claudio in Act 1 Scene 2, where

Lucio speaks almost entirely in prose and is answered by Claudio in verse.

The style of prose in the play displays great variation, for example in the prison scenes where the conversations between Pompey and Barnardine are much less formal than the exchange between the Duke and Escalus. Shakespeare also may have switched between prose and verse as part of his dramatic construction, hoping to achieve different effects upon his audience. (It seems likely that a Jacobean audience was much more likely than a modern one to 'hear' the difference between verse and prose spoken on stage, and to respond differently to each.) The Duke usually speaks in verse, but when he is conversing with Lucio they each use prose. Another revealing example occurs in Act 5: when the Duke is present the dialogue is in verse but when he leaves the stage the characters revert to prose, though the Duke still employs verse even when in disguise as the friar in this act. Perhaps Shakespeare felt that the formality of verse was appropriate to the seriousness of the Duke's position in Act 5.

But it is important to realise that, although prose is less formally or obviously patterned than verse, Shakespeare's prose is nonetheless patterned. It usually possesses, in looser form, the symmetrical features found in verse: rhythm, repetition, imagery, lists, antithesis and balanced phrases and sentences. Within speeches and dialogue, sentences or phrases frequently balance, reflect or oppose each other; for example, the Provost, speaking of Barnardine, describes him as, 'Drunk many times a day, if not many days entirely drunk' (Act 4 Scene 2, lines 131–2).

The verse of *Measure for Measure* is similarly varied, but it is mainly in blank verse: unrhymed verse written in iambic pentameter. It is conventional to define iambic pentameter as the normative pattern of a line with five stressed syllables (/) alternating with five unstressed syllables (×):

    × / × / × / × / × /
    To sue to live, I find I seek to die

At school, Shakespeare had learned the technical definition of iambic pentameter. In Greek *penta* means 'five', and *iamb* means a 'foot' of two syllables, the first unstressed, the second stressed, as in 'alas' = aLAS. Shakespeare practised writing in that metre, and his early plays, such as *Titus Andronicus* or *Richard III*, are very regular in rhythm (often expressed as de-DUM de-DUM de-DUM de-DUM de-DUM), and with each line 'end-stopped' (making sense on its own).

By the time he came to write *Measure for Measure* (in around 1604), Shakespeare had become more flexible and experimental in his use of iambic pentameter. The 'five-beat' metre is still present but less prominent. End-stopped lines are much less frequent. The rhythm of speech is played off against the metrical pattern of the line. There is far greater use of *enjambement* (running on) where one line runs on into the next, seemingly with little or no pause, as in Claudio's speech, 'Ay, but to die' (Act 3 Scene 1, lines 118–32), in which lines run on seamlessly to create a powerful effect.

Shakespeare's use of shorter or longer lines is particularly effective in *Measure for Measure*. Claudio's declaration of courage has a final short line that suggests a pause for emotion or for a gesture, perhaps from Isabella;

If I must die

I will encounter darkness as a bride
And hug it in mine arms.   *(Act 3 Scene 1, lines 82–4)*

The debates between Angelo and Isabella, where they frequently share lines, suggests that there are few pauses in the dialogue, contributing to the impression that they are each passionately engaged in the discussion. In Act 2 Scene 4, Shakespeare also patterns differently the structure of their verse, for example in two pairs of short lines:

ANGELO Then must your brother die.
ISABELLA And 'twere the cheaper way   *(lines 105–6)*

ANGELO Plainly conceive, I love you.
ISABELLA My brother did love Juliet   *(lines 142–3)*

Shakespeare also uses this pattern of echoing short lines to add tension in the exchange in Act 3 Scene 1 between Claudio and Isabella:

CLAUDIO Death is a fearful thing.
ISABELLA And shamèd life a hateful.   *(lines 116–17)*

It seems possible that Shakespeare is suggesting that this reflection of speech patterns is part of Isabella's character, and her ability to 'play with reason and discourse'. This is also evident in the way that she takes a word or words used by another character and changes their emotional weight.

In Act 3 Scene 2, lines 223–44, Shakespeare also gives the Duke a single speech concerning the responsibilities of a ruler. It is written in a different verse form, tetrameter (four-beat metre) rhyming octosyllabic couplets, which effectively draws attention to the themes of the play. Vincentio's speech seems profoundly important to the understanding of Shakespeare's intentions in the play but is dismissed by some critics as an old-fashioned device.

> He who the sword of heaven will bear
> Should be as holy, as severe:
> Pattern in himself to know,
> Grace to stand, and virtue go   *(lines 223–6)*

Some critics, directors and actors have strong convictions about how Shakespeare's verse should be spoken. For example, the director Peter Hall insists there should always be a pause at the end of each line. But it seems appropriate when studying (or watching or acting in) *Measure for Measure* not to attempt to apply rigid rules about verse speaking. Shakespeare certainly used the convention of iambic pentameter, but he did not adhere to it slavishly. He knew 'the rules', but he was not afraid to break them to suit his dramatic purposes. No one knows for sure just how the lines were delivered on Shakespeare's own stage, and today actors use their discretion in how to deliver the lines. They pause or emphasise words to convey meaning and emotion and to avoid the mechanical or clockwork-sounding speech that a too slavish attention to the pentameter line might produce.

Critical approaches

Over the years, critics have viewed *Measure for Measure* in widely differing ways and their own tastes and predilections have necessarily informed their points of view. Recent critical studies have on the whole agreed that *Measure for Measure* is one of Shakespeare's finest plays, profoundly relevant to modern society. What they have radically disagreed about is why this is so. The following section gives you some idea of the widely divergent critical views of *Measure for Measure*.

Traditional criticism

Early commentators on *Measure for Measure* often held the play in low esteem. Dryden, writing in 1672, lumped it together with *Love's Labour's Lost* and *The Winter's Tale* and said they were all, 'either grounded on impossibilities, or at least so meanly written that the comedy neither caused your mirth, nor the serious part your concernment'. The American critic Mrs Charlotte Lennox (1755) felt that Shakespeare contorted the plot 'to bring about three or four weddings, instead of one good beheading'. She admired few of the characters, called Angelo 'cruel . . . vicious and hypocritical' and Isabella 'a mere Vixen in her Virtue' with the 'Manners of an affected Prude'. She has more sympathy for Claudio, describing his 'Desire of Life' as a 'natural Frailty'. She has little time for the Duke: 'His Highness ambles backwards and forwards . . . contriving how to elude those very laws he has been so desirous of having executed.' Mrs Lennox's friend and admirer, Dr Samuel Johnson, wrote that 'the light or comick part is very natural and pleasing, but the grave scenes, if a few passages be excepted, have more labour than elegance. The plot is rather intricate than artful.'

During the early nineteenth century, criticism tended to echo the eighteenth in its comments on what was termed a 'clear moral message'. Hazlitt, writing in 1817, seems to admire Barnardine as 'a fine antithesis to the morality and hypocrisy of the other characters'. He considered the rest of the Viennese low-life characters 'pleasant persons', and he also praised the poetry of parts of the play. Coleridge found the 'pardon and marriage of Angelo . . . degrading to the character of woman'. He said of Pompey the tapster, and the other comic characters in the play, that they 'differ from those of the ignorant and unthinking in general by their superior humour, the poet's own gift and infusion', but in 1827 he changed his opinion. In *Table Talk* he said that '*Measure for Measure* is the single exception to the delightfulness of Shakespeare's plays. It is a hateful work, although Shakespearean throughout. Our feelings of Justice are grossly wounded in Angelo's escape. Isabella herself contrives to be unamiable, and Claudio is detestable.'

Thomas Bowdler approved of parts of the play. Bowdler's claim to fame is that he removed potentially sexual references from all of Shakespeare's plays to produce *The Family Shakespeare* (1818), cutting out all words and phrases that 'cannot with propriety be read aloud in a family'. His name has become synonymous with censorship. He thought that Isabella was admirable and that Angelo was a 'monster of iniquity'. He found *Measure for Measure* almost impossible to 'bowdlerise' as 'the indecent expressions with which many of the scenes abound, are so interwoven with the story, that it is extremely difficult to separate the one from the other'.

Mid nineteenth-century critics tended to idealise Isabella. H N Hudson, in 1848, considered her 'among the finest, in some respects the very finest, of Shakespeare's female characters . . . a saintly anchoress, clad in all the sweet austere composures of womanhood'. In 1863, Charles Cowden Clarke refutes earlier criticisms of Isabella: 'I think it a reproach upon men that they should treat injuriously one of the most beautiful-souled among Shakespeare's beautifully-souled women.'

Later nineteenth- and early twentieth-century critics frequently viewed *Measure for Measure* as an artistic failure, partly because they tried to force it into a specific category and then complained when it did not fit existing genres (comedy, tragedy or history). In 1896, the critic F S Boas invented the term 'problem play' as an innovative genre to include *Measure for Measure*, *Troilus and Cressida* and *All's Well That Ends Well*. That label has tended to stick to the play (together with 'problem comedy' or 'dark comedy') because critics have felt it is not a tragedy, but yet is too serious to fit the conventionally accepted category of comedy. But in recent years, many critics have tended to avoid the concept 'problem play' because they argue that few other Shakespeare plays can be categorised into such simple genres as comedy or tragedy.

In his influential study, *The Wheel of Fire* (published in 1930), G Wilson Knight felt that the central theme of the play is 'the moral nature of man in relation to the crudity of man's justice, especially in the matter of sexual vice'. He claimed that 'the ethical standards of the Gospels are rooted in *Measure for Measure*' and that the play 'tends towards allegory or symbolism', specifically Christian allegory. Using an analysis more commonly applied to medieval plays he states that:

> Isabella stands for sainted purity, Angelo for Pharisaical righteousness, the Duke for a psychologically sound and enlightened ethic. Lucio represents indecent wit, Pompey and Mistress Overdone professional immorality. Barnardine is hardheaded, criminal insensitiveness. Each person illustrates some facet of the central theme: man's moral nature.

Wilson Knight argues that the subject of the play is 'sexual ethics', which he claims presents a 'contrast between human consciousness and human instinct; so rigid a distinction between the civilized and the natural qualities of man; so amazing, yet so slight, a boundary set in the public mind between the foully bestial and the ideally divine in humanity'. At the centre of Wilson Knight's analysis of the play is his interpretation of the role of the Duke:

> He controls the action from start to finish, he allots as it were, praise and blame, he is lit at moments with divine suggestion comparable with his almost divine power of fore-knowledge, and control, and wisdom. There is an enigmatic other-worldly, mystery suffusing his figure and the meaning of his acts: their result, however, in each case justifies their initiation – wherein we see the allegorical nature of the play, since the plot is so arranged that each person received his deserts in the light of the Duke's – which is really the Gospel – ethic.

Knight's uncritical enthusiasm for the Duke is unbounded, and stands in stark contrast to many recent assessments of Vincentio's character and intentions. He justifies his radically Christian reading of the Duke by pointing to Angelo's reference in Act 5 Scene 1, line 362 to the Duke's knowledge of his actions, 'like power divine', and by a reference to the Duke's rhyming couplets at the end of Act 3 Scene 2, commenting that 'The Duke, like Jesus, is the prophet of a new order of ethics':

> He who the sword of heaven will bear
> Should be as holy, as severe   *(Act 3 Scene 2, lines 223–4)*

In contrast to the many other critics who feel that Act 5 of *Measure for Measure* presents problems of interpretation, Wilson Knight asserts that: 'The varied close-inwoven themes of *Measure for Measure* are finally knit in the exquisite final act' where all the characters are 'summoned to the final judgement'.

Wilson Knight's study of Isabella focuses on what he calls her 'self-centred saintliness'. He judges that she lacks 'human feeling' and declares that her rejection of Claudio's plea for life is pressed 'like a fiend'. He thinks that Isabella's failure is greater than Angelo's:

> Her sex inhibitions have been horribly shown her as they are, naked. She has been stung – lanced on a sore spot of her soul. She knows now that it is not all saintliness, she sees her own soul and sees it as something small, frightened, despicable, too frail to dream of such a sacrifice . . . Isabella, however, was no hypocrite, any more than Angelo. She is a spirit of purity, grace, maiden charm: but all these virtues the action of the play turns remorselessly against herself.

Yet Knight concedes that, as the play proceeds, and as Isabella finally agrees to plea for Angelo's life, she moves from 'sanctity to humanity'. Similarly, he grants eventual humanity to Angelo, who, Knight argues, 'aimed too high when he cast his eyes on the sainted Isabel: now, knowing himself, he will find his true level in the love of Mariana'. He concludes by suggesting that *Measure for Measure* must be read 'as a parable', like the parables of Jesus. He concludes his strongly Christian reading of *Measure for Measure* with:

> But, in truth, no play of Shakespeare shows more thoughtful care, more deliberate purpose, more consummate skill in structural technique, and, finally, more penetrating ethical and psychological insight. None shows a more exquisitely inwoven pattern. And, if ever the thought at first sight seems strange, or

the action unreasonable, it will be ever found to reflect the
sublime strangeness and unreason of Jesus' teaching.

Writing in 1979, Darryl J Gless argues very powerfully that *Measure
for Measure* is not a religious allegory, but that it is informed by the
religious atmosphere of the times in which it was written. He asserts
that Shakespeare is 'using conventions of language and meaning; he
is not necessarily voicing personal beliefs'. Looking at earlier critics of
the play, Gless divides them into those who think that *Measure for
Measure* embodies central concepts of Christian doctrine, and those
who do not. Generalising, he assumes that the critics who favour
Christian interpretations 'encourage favourable assessments of the
play's aesthetic integrity'. Anti-Christian interpretations do not. Much
of Gless' analysis of the play depends on a detailed analysis of St
Matthew's Gospel, in particular the 'Sermon on the Mount' and on the
Christian doctrine of charitable love. He also draws attention to the
Roman Catholic references surrounding Isabella's entry into the order
of the Poor Clares, reminding the reader of the anti-Catholic feeling in
Elizabethan and Jacobean England. Monastic life, and chastity in
particular, were matters of current and raging controversy at the time.
Gless remarks that 'Such fugitive and cloistered virtue was very much
at odds with the humanistic bent of Shakespeare's age.'

In an article equally concerned with the ethical design of the play,
but far less overtly Christian in tone, L C Knights begins, 'It is
probably true to say that *Measure for Measure* is that play of
Shakespeare's which has caused most readers the greatest sense of
strain and mental discomfort.' He claims that the main impulse of the
action is 'of course the sexual instinct', and that Angelo and Mistress
Overdone 'represent the extremes of suppression and licence'.
However, although he thinks that Angelo is 'the admitted success of
the play', Knights judges him, 'a sketch rather than a developed
character study'. For Knights, the 'problem' of *Measure for Measure* lies
in the function of the character of Claudio, whom he claims is
'scarcely a "character" at all'. Knights compares the way various
attitudes to sexuality are expressed in the play, pointing out that only
Isabella and Angelo feel that Claudio has committed a sin. Lucio, the
Provost, and even Escalus think that his offence is 'venial' and does
not deserve the death sentence. But on the theme of liberty and
restraint, and the question of justice being done, Knights is critical of

how the play resolves these issues. He claims that 'it is significant that the last two acts, showing obvious signs of haste, are little more than a drawing out and resolution of the plot . . . but the problems remain'. Unlike his judgement that Shakespeare's other great plays offer 'clarification', Knights is sceptical that Shakespeare achieves that here. He concludes that 'In *Measure for Measure* the process of clarification is incomplete, and one finds not paradox but genuine ambiguity.'

F R Leavis, writing in *Scrutiny* in 1942, takes issue with L C Knights, feeling that Knights has 'imported into *Measure for Measure* something that wasn't put there by Shakespeare'. He interprets Claudio's own attitude to his offence as unsurprising, 'that he should be bitterly self-reproachful and self-condemnatory, and impute a heavier guilt to himself than anyone else (except Isabella and Angelo) imputes to him, is surely natural'. He suggests that Knights is influenced by the 'accepted classing of *Measure for Measure* with the "unpleasant" and "pessimistic" "problem" plays'. About Isabella, Leavis writes, 'we surely know that her attitude is not Shakespeare's, and is not meant to be ours'. On the other hand he does think that the Duke's attitude 'is meant to be ours – his total attitude, which is the total attitude of the play'.

Leavis concludes that 'It is Shakespeare's great triumph in *Measure for Measure* to have achieved so inclusive and delicate complexity, and to have shown us complexity distinguished from contradiction, conflict and uncertainty, with so sure and subtle a touch.'

Elizabeth M Pope, writing in 1982, considers that it is of primary importance to understand the theological and ethical atmosphere of Shakespeare's own time. She points out that the idea of judgement was a current contemporary debate; and that, while the doctrine of judgement expressed in the Gospels was accepted, the point that was debated was – just who should exact that judgement? As the king was God's substitute on earth, it should be the king. She points out that 'Any Renaissance audience would have taken it for granted that the Duke did indeed "stand for" God, but only as any good ruler "stood for" Him; and if he behaved "like power divine", it was because that was the way a good ruler was expected to conduct himself.' He was expected to use 'craft against vice' following the advice King James gives to his son in *Basilicon Doron*. She draws attention to the paradox inherent in the power of the king. Her argument is that though the king had god-like attributes as ruler, he was 'only man "dressed in a little brief authority" . . . whom his God will in the end call strictly to account, although his subjects may not'. Pope also draws attention to another contemporary debate running through the play, which she identifies as the extent to which justice should be tempered by mercy. She concludes by stating that Shakespeare

> sheds no light on his own denominational preferences; he touches in this play only on such elements of traditional theology as were shared by Anglican, Puritan and Roman Catholic alike. Nor, since to dramatise a doctrine is not necessarily to believe in it, are we entitled to use *Measure for Measure* as evidence that he himself was a Christian.

E M W Tillyard argues strongly that *Measure for Measure* 'changes nature half-way through', which he ascribes to the way that Shakespeare has used his source material:

> The simple and ineluctable fact is that the tone in the first half of the play is frankly, acutely human and quite hostile to the tone of allegory or symbol. And however much the tone changes in the second half, nothing in the world can make an allegorical interpretation poetically valid throughout.

His major criticism is that the change that he identifies at Act 3 Scene 1, line 152 is one of literary style. Tillyard extends his criticism of the inconsistency of the play further to the interpretation of character. He complains that the Duke is a minor character in the first half, 'with no influence on the way human motives are presented', but becomes 'the dominant character in the second half and the one through whose mind human motives are judged'. Isabella he describes as, 'not, dramatically, the same Isabella' in the second half of the play as in the first: 'Whether in the second half Shakespeare reverted to an original plan from which he had played truant, or whether he began to improvise when he found himself stuck, we shall never know.'

David Lloyd Stevenson in *The Achievement of Shakespeare's Measure for Measure* justifies the change in tone identified by critics such as E M W Tillyard: 'It is because *Measure for Measure* is structured as an intellectual counterpoise of moral concepts and ideas that the normal, tragic results of the actions and decisions of the chief characters are suspended in favour of coldly comic irony and paradox.' Stevenson denies that the play 'endorses' Christian theological assertions, though he does think that it uses them dramatically: 'Finally, if we follow Knight, Chambers, Coghill and company in feeling that we must read *Measure for Measure* as a parable with a lesson driven home, or as a play at least strongly buttressed with special Christian teachings, we are left with a serious aesthetic problem.' Stevenson's view is that the play will be seen to be successful dramatically in giving 'a sharper recognition of the complex nature of problems of moral decision'. He feels that this is what makes it relevant to a modern audience irrespective of an understanding of its historical context.

In *Shakespeare's Imagery and What It Tells Us*, Caroline Spurgeon opened up a further critical perspective on *Measure for Measure*: the study of its imagery. It should be noted that although later critics have acknowledged the value of Caroline Spurgeon's pioneering study of Shakespeare's imagery, her work has also been much criticised. For example, she underestimates the amount of imagery in *Measure for Measure*, totally ignores all its sexual imagery, and only occasionally examines how the imagery relates to the dramatic context of the play. She has also been criticised for her flowery style and her invariable tone of praise, avoiding any critical appraisal of the play's imagery. She describes *Measure for Measure* as 'that strange play which holds so much of Shakespeare's deepest thought'. In her analysis of the imagery she singles out the Duke's speeches as containing some of the 'most beautiful as well as the most thoughtful similes in the whole of Shakespeare' and 'many of the most brilliant and unusual of Shakespeare's pictures and personifications'. Spurgeon classifies many of the images as 'vivid, quaint, or grotesque' rather than 'poetic', and she comments on the striking pictures evoked by personification, for example: 'Liberty plucks Justice by the nose'. She also notes in the play 'what is, even for Shakespeare, an unusually vivid use of concrete verbs and adjectives', for example:

> Hooking both right and wrong to th'appetite
> To follow as it draws   *(Act 2 Scene 4, lines 177–8)*

> Lent him our terror, dressed him with our love
> *(Act 1 Scene 1, line 19)*

                              a purpose
        More grave and wrinkled than the aims and ends
        Of burning youth.   *(Act 1 Scene 3, lines 4–6)*

In a detailed historical investigation of the play, *The Problem of Measure for Measure*, Rosalind Miles draws the conclusion that while many of the plays' analysts find fault with the characterisation of the Duke, it 'may be rehabilitated by an effort of the historical imagination'. In her study she places *Measure for Measure* very precisely within its historical context, comparing other playwrights' work, and Shakespeare's own use of plot devices, themes, structures and characters in other plays with those of *Measure for Measure*. She says that it may be 'one of the rare plays which does not provide any clear point of reference for its audience. This lack of a fixed centre is one of the reasons why *Measure for Measure* is such a problematical drama, and why so many contrasting and contradictory interpretations are possible.' Miles concludes: '*Measure for Measure* remains an only partially successful play.'

Modern criticism

Throughout the second half of the twentieth century, and in the twenty-first, critical approaches to Shakespeare have radically challenged the style and assumptions of the traditional approaches described above. New critical approaches argue that traditional interpretations, with their focus on character and personal feelings, are individualistic and misleading. They ignore society and history, and so divorce literary, dramatic and aesthetic matters from their social context. Furthermore, their detachment from the real world makes them elitist, sexist and unpolitical.

Modern critical perspectives therefore shift the focus from studying characters as individuals to assessing their dramatic contexts, and to looking at how social conditions (of the world of the play and of Shakespeare's England) are reflected in characters' relationships, language and behaviour. Modern criticism also concerns itself with how changing social assumptions at different periods of time have affected interpretations of *Measure for Measure*.

The following discussion is organised under headings that represent major contemporary critical perspectives (political, feminist, performance, psychoanalytic, post-modern), but it is vital to appreciate that there is often overlap between the categories and that to pigeonhole any example of criticism too precisely is to reduce its value and application.

Political criticism

'Political criticism' is a convenient label for approaches concerned with power and social structure in the world of the play, in Shakespeare's time and in our own. It takes many different forms, but each is concerned with political relationships: between the powerful and the powerless; between men and women; between the state and its desire to control all aspects of social life, and between the political power men hold and their temptations and moral weaknesses in exercising that power. The problem of a duke who suddenly abandons power and is replaced by the 'corrupt deputy' is at the heart of the play.

Jonathan Dollimore questions the traditional view that in Vienna, anarchy, through unrestrained sexuality, threatens to overwhelm the state. He takes the political view that early critics have accepted unquestioningly, that 'sexual transgression in *Measure for Measure* – and in the world – represents a real force of social disorder intrinsic to human nature and that the play at least is about how this force is – must be – restrained'. He writes that the literary theorist Mikhail Bakhtin's analysis of the 'subversive carnivalesque' invites a reading of *Measure for Measure* that 'interprets the low-life transgression as *positively* anarchic, ludic, carnivalesque – a subversion from below of a repressive official ideology of order'. (Bakhtin and his circle stated that language has no fixed meanings but is endlessly redefined in use.)

In his reading of the play, Dollimore claims that *Measure for Measure* is about the authorities' fear of the threat posed by any deviancy, and 'like many apparent threats to authority this one legitimises it'. He feels that *Measure for Measure* invokes the problems of Jacobean London and the authorities' fear of vagabonds and masterless men: 'Yet, if anything *Measure for Measure* emphasises the lack of any coherent opposition among the subordinate and marginalised. Thus Pompey . . . once imprisoned and with the promise of remission, becomes, with no sense of betrayal, servant to the State in no less a capacity than that of hangman.' Dollimore comments on the way that Escalus accuses Isabella of being suborned by 'some more mightier member' and he is prepared to torture to discover the potential threat. Dollimore writes: 'At the same time we can read in that anxiety – in its very surplus, its imaginative intensity, its punitive ingenuity – an ideological displacement (and hence misrecognition) of much deeper fears of the uncontrollable, of being out of control, themselves corresponding to more fundamental social problems.' He concludes:

> the transgressors in *Measure for Measure* signify neither the unregeneracy of the flesh, nor the ludic subversive carnivalesque. Rather, as the spectre of unregulated desire, they are exploited to legitimate an exercise in authoritarian repression.

Writing in 1988, Marc Shell argues that *Measure for Measure* does not refer to the Bible for instruction about fornication, but to politics and the 'teleological consequences of fornication in the political order'. By focusing on Claudio and Juliet's pregnancy, rather than the professional fornicators who escape the ultimate punishment, the play is less about the political control of sexuality than the restriction of reproduction. He also notes that in Act 3 Scene 1, when the Duke as friar takes over the management of the plot, he also takes over from Angelo the role of wooer of Isabella. Shell writes that, from the beginning of the play 'the injunction to increase comes not from God but from nature':

> the collision of two motive forces powers the plot of *Measure for Measure*. On the one hand is the urge to reproduce our own kind, no matter how; on the other is the urge to set limits on how we reproduce or to arrest reproduction altogether. In no other work that I know are these issues so extended to their logical, dramaturgical, and anthropological limits.

In *Recycling Shakespeare*, Charles Marowitz writes: 'No-one treated women with more exquisite cruelty than Shakespeare.' He sums up the plot of *Measure for Measure* from Isabella's point of view:

> Isabella is wrenched from the cloister, threatened with sexual abuse by Angelo, and made to feel morally responsible for the imminent execution of her brother. After being talked into a humiliating sexual substitution with Angelo's former

betrothed, she is put into the moral predicament of pleading to save the life of the man who tried to ravish her. This plea granted, she is coolly appropriated by the Duke, without regard to her own wishes.

Marowitz has rewritten the play, taking out the 'bed-trick' (Isabella yields to Angelo); he omits the comedy scenes with Pompey, Elbow and Mistress Overdone; Claudio is beheaded, and the Duke supports Angelo for reasons of policy. In Marowitz's final scene, the Duke decides to 'appropriate' Isabella for himself. She has already slept with Angelo and is therefore 'damaged goods'. As she runs from the Duke, she runs into Angelo, flees from him into the arms of Lucio, then she finds her way blocked by a reincarnated lustful Claudio, and all four men move in on her as the lights fade. Marowitz makes the point that 'Throughout, Isabella has been the helpless pawn of the law, and the excruciating irony is that it was to the law that she had turned first for clemency and then redress.'

Terry Eagleton, writing in 1986, also focuses on the political and moral implications of law: 'That anarchy and authoritarianism are not quite the contraries they seem is made dramatically obvious in *Measure for Measure* by Angelo's sudden about-turn from repressive legalist to rampant lecher.' His argument is that when a system of 'purely abstract or formal law . . . becomes detached from desire . . . law actually *breeds* desire as well as blocks it':

> The law is not simply repressive, a negative prohibition placed upon the will; what is desired is precisely what is most strictly tabooed, and the taboo perversely intensifies the yearning. It is Isabella's chaste untouchability which fuels Angelo's passion, so that desire and prohibition become mutually ensnared, apparent opposites which are in truth secret conditions of one another.

Eagleton defends Isabella's refusal to sacrifice her virginity for Claudio's life by suggesting that if she does so then she will be compromising a principle: 'Just as a particular commercial bargain may alter the general rates of exchange which govern it, so more than one woman's virginity is at stake in turning down Angelo's deal.' He argues that the play celebrates mercy, but not the negative indifference of Lucio or Barnardine:

How is Mercy to break the vicious circle of prosecutions when it must somehow spring from inside that circle, from a humble solidarity with vice? If that censorious circularity is indeed transformable into a community of mutual acceptance, from what vantage-point – inside or beyond the circuit, or at its very edge – can this be effected? These are not, finally, questions which the play can satisfactorily answer.

Feminist criticism

Feminist criticism is part of the wider cause of feminism, which aims to achieve rights and equality for women in social, political and economic life. It challenges sexism: those beliefs and practices that result in the degradation, oppression and subordination of women. Feminist criticism therefore challenges traditional portrayals of female characters as examples of 'virtue' or 'vice'. It rejects 'male ownership' of criticism in which men determine what questions are to be asked of a play, and which answers are acceptable. Feminism argues that male criticism often neglects, represses or mis-represents female experience, and stereotypes or distorts women's points of view.

Given that *Measure for Measure* is centrally concerned with sexual politics, it is a little surprising that there has been comparatively little feminist criticism of a play where powerless women figure as neurotic, sexually inhibited novice nuns, forsaken lovers, bawds and prostitutes. Men so obviously hold all the power, and use it to reinforce the negative stereotyping of women. Even at the play's end, the position of the women remains subordinate, or at best ambiguous.

In *Shakespeare and the Nature of Women*, Juliet Dusinberre finds much to admire in Shakespeare's presentation of women, suggesting that he challenges the gender stereotyping of his time. She writes of Shakespeare's awareness of the way that 'Men and women perform on stage the gender roles which they are required to perform in society, thus highlighting the theatricality inherent in their social behaviour.' Though she draws attention to the 'friar's' comment to Juliet that her sin was 'of heavier kind' than Claudio's, Dusinberre feels that the Duke as friar is expressing the official view of the Church, and that *Measure for Measure* does not accept that chastity is mainly for women. She comments:

If Isabella acquiesces in Angelo's proposal she sells her virginity for tangible gain as the whore does. But the terms of her repudiation of him underwrite the ethical assumption that a woman's only virtue is her chastity. Isabella's virginity has a rateable value 'More than our brother is our chastity'. Despite her indignant purity, she assesses herself by the world's standards. Mariana, a creature judged soiled by the world, is more independent of it, espousing other-worldly values; the charity of the dispossessed . . . Generosity, compassion, tolerance are not present in Isabella's rigorous chastity. They develop in a woman who can see the limits of the world's judgement of women.

Dusinberre suggests that 'Renaissance drama places in a hostile environment women whose education renders them as eloquent and as rational as men.' She goes on to look at the exchange offered to Mariana by the Duke, who gives her nominal marriage to Angelo so that she may become a wealthy widow, 'implying that cash in this instance might actually be a better bargain than Angelo'.

Lisa Jardine rejects Dusinberre's view. She argues that, 'the strong interest in women shown by Elizabethan and Jacobean drama does not in fact reflect newly improved social conditions, and a greater possibility for women, but rather is relative to the patriarchy's unexpressed worry about the great social changes which characterise the period – worries which could be made conveniently concrete in the voluminous and endemic debates about "the woman question"'. In *Still Harping on Daughters*, Jardine writes about the various literary stereotypes of virtuous young women. She comments on Isabella's dilemma in *Measure for Measure*, suggesting that she, 'most complicatedly incorporates the full range of possibilities latent in these admirably steadfast and courageous assaulted (or at least slandered) women'. She also draws attention to the fact that in a play dealing largely with sexual activity, only Angelo and Isabella seem to feel guilt for their sexuality:

And in this context, I think, the expectations concerning saintly virgins whose virtue is assaulted are used to undermine Isabella's position during the crucial scenes in which she allows her brother to go to his death, rather than submit to Angelo.

Were Isabella Lucretia (and the similarities between the preliminary circumstances are extremely close in the two stories), she would submit to enforced sex, tell all afterwards, and kill herself. That is what patriarchy expects of a female hero under such circumstances.

Because Isabella refuses to conform to the expected pattern of behaviour, Jardine feels that 'her virtue is placed in question'. Quoting Claudio's plea to Isabella she points out that, in the traditional expectations of women's behaviour, he is right:

> Sweet sister, let me live.
> What sin you do to save a brother's life,
> Nature dispenses with the deed so far
> That it becomes a virtue.   *(Act 3 Scene 1, lines 133–6)*

Kathleen McLuskie's analysis of *Measure for Measure* discusses the fact that the images of the women are presented through masculine opinions, and she asserts that 'The confusion in the narrative meaning is created because it offers equal dramatic power to mutually exclusive positions.' She defines this as the way that the 'comic vitality' of the presentation of the low-life characters, and their resistance to the restraint of law, is opposed by the Duke's passionate expression of disgust at their 'filthy vice'. She writes: 'Similarly Isabella's single-minded protection of her sexual autonomy is placed first by the masochism of the sexual imagery in which it is expressed and then by its juxtaposition with her brother's equally vividly expressed terror at the thought of death.' McLuskie concludes:

> Feminist criticism of this play is restricted to exposing its own exclusion from the text. It has no point of entry into it, for the dilemmas of the narrative and the sexuality under discussion are constructed in completely male terms – gelding and splaying hold no terror for women – and the women's role as the objects of exchange within that system of sexuality is not at issue, however much a feminist might want to draw attention to it. Thus when a feminist accepts the narrative, theatrical and intellectual pleasures of this text she does so in male terms and not as part of the locus of feminist critical activity.

Performance criticism

Performance criticism fully acknowledges that *Measure for Measure* is a play: a script to be performed by actors to an audience. It examines all aspects of the play in performance: its staging in the theatre or on film and video. Performance criticism focuses on Shakespeare's stagecraft and the semiotics of theatre (words, costumes, gestures, etc.), together with the 'afterlife' of the play (what happened to *Measure for Measure* after Shakespeare wrote it). That involves scrutiny of how productions at different periods have presented the play, and how the text has been cut, added to, rewritten and rearranged to present a version felt appropriate to the times. The first recorded performance of *Measure for Measure* was during the 1604–5 Christmas festivities of King James' court. There were eleven plays during the celebrations, seven of which were by Shakespeare. After the Restoration, William Davenant, who claimed to have been Shakespeare's natural son, adapted *Measure for Measure* in 1662 to suit the popular taste for lively plays with music and dancing. He combined the main plot with the Beatrice and Benedick episodes of *Much Ado About Nothing* and called it *The Law Against Lovers*. Samuel Pepys saw it performed and commented in his diary that it was, 'a good play and well performed, especially the little girl's (whom I never saw act before) dancing and singing'. (The 'little girl' was playing Beatrice's sister.) In 1700, Charles Gildon rewrote a version of *Measure for Measure*, which he called *Beauty the Best Advocate*. In it, Angelo is offered as a birthday present Purcell's opera *Dido and Aeneas*, arranged as a court entertainment. John Philip Kemble produced an acting version of the play in 1795. Most of the obscene references were taken out and it was heavily cut: Act 4 Scene 1 was entirely removed because Isabella's discussion of the 'bed-trick' was felt to be indelicate. Where Kemble felt that Shakespeare had missed some opportunities for clearing up the ending, he added speeches and stage directions to make everything tidy.

Measure for Measure was relatively unpopular in Victorian times and rarely performed, partly because it offended conventional sensibilities. William Poel (1852–1934) was the first director to stage all three 'problem plays', and his work was extremely influential in encouraging the reappraisal of these plays. But it was not until the second half of the twentieth century that *Measure for Measure* was fully acknowledged in performance as one of Shakespeare's major achievements. Its troubled plot and characters have increasingly been seen as reflecting the sceptical, uncertain, complex nature of modern society.

Jonathan Miller's 1975 production divested the play of much of the potentially religious aura. Isabella was played as a deliberately unsexual fervent nun, whose very harshness attracted Angelo. Miller had Isabella recoil in horror at the Duke's proposal. In the Players of Shakespeare series (published by Cambridge University Press) there are fascinating accounts from the actors' points of view. These include Daniel Massey's and Roger Allam's accounts of their exploration of the character of the Duke for the Royal Shakespeare Company's productions of 1983 and 1987 respectively. They write of the challenges involved in playing a major character who has no self-revelatory soliloquies, taking the reader through the process of creating a character from the script. In *Clamorous Voices – Shakespeare's Women Today*, Carol Rutter records two major female actors, Paola Dionisotti and Juliet Stevenson, speaking about their very different experiences of playing Isabella. It is particularly interesting to compare Juliet Stevenson's perspective with Daniel Massey's as they played Isabella and the Duke in the same production. They chose to show a growing affection between the Duke and Isabella, developing from their first meeting. There was a touching moment at the jail when the Duke tells Isabella that Claudio is dead. The Duke comforted her. They made eye contact, and seemed to be about to kiss, when Lucio arrived. He watched them for a moment, then drawled sarcastically, 'Good even; friar, where's the provost?' This made them spring apart guiltily, which earned a laugh from the audience. The end of Act 5 was memorable, as Isabella seemed relieved that she had not fallen in love with a friar, Angelo seemed repentant and grateful for Mariana's fidelity, Claudio and Juliet joyfully displayed their new baby and Lucio's punishment was comic. The Royal Shakespeare Company's 1987 production led to a much bleaker ending: Angelo seemed to resent marriage to Mariana; his demand for, 'Immediate sentence then, and sequent death' appeared to be heartfelt. Isabella seemed appalled by the proposal from the Duke and stood irresolute. The reactions of other characters to the punishment of Lucio made it appear harsher. Only Claudio and Juliet were embracing.

In 2001, in a BBC Radio 3 talk, 'Shakespeare is Dead', the director Michael Bogdanov said that the question the audience should be asking is, 'Why does the scumbag Duke get the girl?' His 1985 production for the Stratford Festival in Canada exemplified his approach. It prefixed the production with a 30-minute cabaret suggesting the decadence of Vienna. In his Act 1 he transposed Scenes 2 and 3 to bring the focus more precisely on the Duke, who was played as a fop, worried about his appearance. Bogdanov's production focused on the politics and power-struggle in the play. The theatre critic, Richard Hillman, described the final act of this production:

> It is a triumphant fifth act self-staging, the culmination of his meta-dramatic manoeuvres is precisely calculated to rally 'loud applause and aves vehement' in support of the Duke's return to re-incarnate what Claudio cynically terms 'the demi-god, Authority' (Act 1 Scene 2, line 102). This point was stressed to brilliant theatrical effect . . . in which the ruler in the guise of a contemporary military dictator, with dark glasses and armed guards, arrived by helicopter and displayed himself on a balcony to the accompaniment of deafening cheers and dazzling flashbulbs.

Stephen Boxer, who played Angelo in the 1997 Royal Shakespeare Company production, thinks that to have the Duke rejected by Isabella is a cynical way of directing the end of the play, and is much more in favour of a redemptive approach: 'It is very pertinent now – the notion of redemption. I think intellectually we often want it, but emotionally we find it very difficult . . . It has always been a problem about what you do with a penal system, whether we believe in rehabilitation or if we just believe in shutting our eyes and cutting people off. Because we have a fundamentally Christian ethos, the issue of redemption still keeps coming back to haunt us.' Boxer also makes an interesting point about Shakespeare's presentation of Angelo:

> He is the most corrupted character and yet Shakespeare allows him to share his thoughts with the audience. There is an element in which you think, well Shakespeare knows that there but by the grace of God, maybe, go a lot of us – so you sense from that a sympathy for the character even in his most blackened, disgraceful moments.

The celebrated director John Barton, speaking about directing *Measure for Measure*, has said: 'If one is rehearsing *Measure for Measure* rather than just studying it, one has to answer questions about what the Duke's really like, and what's going on inside him, and that leads to finding out about a human being rather than defining an allegory. It has often been said that, on reading the play, one finds it splitting down the middle. At the point Isabella leaves Claudio after her interview with him in the prison, and is left alone with the Duke, the level of writing changes . . . in the theatre, I think that the difference disappears. This is because the actors, if they have brought their characters to life in exploring the first half, can carry through that life into the play's more superficial resolution.'

In his influential study *Speechless Dialect*, written in 1985, Philip C McGuire examines Shakespeare's use of silence on stage. McGuire explores five different productions of *Measure for Measure* and considers that the play provides the most challenging and complex example of Shakespeare's use of 'open silence'. He identifies six characters who remain silent at the end of the play: Angelo, who speaks only once when he is brought back on stage after his marriage to Mariana to request his own execution; Barnardine, who does not respond verbally to his pardon from the Duke; Claudio and Juliet, who say nothing when they are reunited in the final scene; and Mariana and Juliet, whose last words are to request that the Duke should extend mercy to Angelo. McGuire points out that these silences are made more noticeable in relation to Lucio's 'irrepressible garrulousness'.

> Each of those six silences is open, and each of them can alter an audience's sense of the moral vision of *Measure for Measure*. As the implications and impacts of those silences vary from production to production, the play's perspective upon a host of issues shifts accordingly. Those issues, several of which continue to trouble and divide societies to this day, include the role of deception in the act of governing, the proper exercise and the limits of civil power, the relationship between mercy and human systems of justice, the morality of capital punishment, the wisdom of using law to control sexual behaviour, the conflicting desires to engage in and to withdraw from a sordid world, and the interplay between

legal authority and erotic love in the institution of marriage. The openness of each of these separate silences deepens and becomes more extensive because of the groupings that emerge from them.

McGuire points out that, of the four men under sentence of death on stage, all are spared but only one speaks, Lucio, and that the 'interplay of words spoken and silences' draws attention to the power of language in *Measure for Measure*. He points to the fact that 'whoever is the voice of Viennese law can, by phrasing words into sentences, take or bestow human life. "Mortality and mercy in Vienna / Live in thy tongue and heart", the Duke tells Angelo on appointing him deputy'. Comparing different productions, McGuire notes that the behaviour and attitude of the silent Barnardine on stage can either affirm the Duke's power and mercy or suggest their limits.

None of those who are, or are to be, married at the end of *Measure for Measure* exchange any verbal expressions of love, and that 'generates a field of possible effects and meanings as wide and complex as those arising from the silences of those who receive life from the Duke'. The two men who are reprieved by the Duke, Angelo and Lucio, are condemned to marriage by the Duke. Lucio considers that his new sentence is heavier: 'Marrying a punk, my lord, is pressing to death, whipping, and hanging!' Angelo only speaks once after he is married, and says, 'I crave death more willingly than mercy'. Comparing his words to Mariana's when she pleads for Angelo's life, 'I crave no other, nor no better man', McGuire comments, 'The repetition of "crave" underscores that what Mariana wants is precisely what Angelo has no desire to be: a living man who is her husband. What Angelo expressly asks for with the last words he utters is death, but what he receives from the Duke is life, and it is life with a woman to whom he never again speaks.'

McGuire also remarks that the last words between Claudio and Isabella are in the prison cell in Act 3 (Scene 1), where Isabella declares that she will speak 'No word to save thee'. The fact that Claudio is entirely silent in the final scene and that Isabella does not speak to him is all the more striking because she has been so eloquent in her verbal defence of Angelo. When the Duke pardons Claudio he also asks Isabella to be his wife: 'Give me your hand, and say you will be mine', but here too she does not speak.

The Duke's words pardoning Claudio, proposing to Isabella, and instructing Angelo to love his wife are embedded within as many as five silences: Isabella's toward the Duke, Angelo's toward Mariana, Claudio's toward both Isabella and Juliet, and . . . Barnardine's. Each of these silences is open to a range of meanings and effects, and the interplay among the silences generates a cumulative openness that is even more challenging. The result is a theatrical moment strikingly rich in possibilities.

McGuire goes on to examine in detail a range of interpretations in five different productions of *Measure for Measure*, discussing the wide variety of possibilities that Shakespeare has given to the director in these 'open silences'. By describing the actions of the actors, he demonstrates how different positions on stage, responses, gestures and body language can radically alter the meaning of the end of the play and its effects on the audience.

He concludes that the 'six open silences' of the final scene of *Measure for Measure* give the play 'an extraordinary freedom, a capacity for contingency and change unmatched by any other Shakespearean play with the possible exception of *King Lear*. We cannot even be certain what kind of play *Measure for Measure* is'. McGuire feels that *Measure for Measure* 'may be a comedy but does not have to be':

Measure for Measure must always pose problems for those who equate the play with the words that Shakespeare wrote, who seek to make the play conform to the words that are a major part of it. Those words establish the presence of open silences that require the play, during its final moments, to move beyond and float free of its verbal elements. As it ends, *Measure for Measure* defies easy categorisation as a comedy and mutely but insistently asserts its identity as a drama.

Psychoanalytic criticism

In the 20th century, psychoanalysis became a major influence on the understanding and interpretation of human behaviour. The founder of psychoanalysis, Sigmund Freud, explained personality as the result of unconscious and irrational desires, repressed memories or wishes, sexuality, fantasy, anxiety and conflict. Freud's theories have had a strong influence on criticism and stagings of Shakespeare's plays, most obviously on *Hamlet* in the well-known claim that Hamlet suffers from an Oedipus complex. Freudian interpretations of *Measure for Measure* tend to focus on Angelo and Isabella particularly (both as intensely psychically repressed characters), and sometimes on the Duke. Critics refer to Angelo's latent sadism, 'Hoping you'll find good cause to whip them all' (Act 2 Scene 1, line 121), and on Isabella's unconsciously masochistic imagery in her refusal to accept a sexual proposition:

> were I under the terms of death,
> Th'impression of keen whips I'd wear as rubies,
> And strip myself to death as to a bed
> That longing have been sick for, ere I'd yield
> My body up to shame.   *(Act 2 Scene 4, lines 100–4)*

Other critics who are psychoanalytically inclined have argued for an incest motif in the 'bed-trick' with the girl in the dark as the 'tabooed mother'. Others have focused on Angelo's unconscious desires; or on the guilt experienced for merely thinking of crimes; and on the Duke as representing the superego. There has even been an extraordinary cannibalistic interpretation (sparked by Isabella's saying her brother is not prepared for death).

Such interpretations reveal the obvious weaknesses in applying psychoanalytic theories to *Measure for Measure*. They are highly speculative, and can be neither proved nor disproved. Psychoanalytic approaches are therefore often accused of imposing interpretations based on theory rather than upon Shakespeare's text. Nonetheless, the play has obvious features which seem to invite psychoanalytic approaches: the desire to restrain sexuality, an attempted rape, sadism and masochism.

Postmodern criticism
Postmodern criticism (sometimes called 'deconstruction') is not always easy to understand because it is not centrally concerned with consistency or reasoned argument. It does not accept that one section of the story is necessarily connected to what follows, or that characters relate to each other in meaningful ways. The approach therefore has obvious drawbacks in providing a model for examination students

who are expected to display reasoned, coherent argument, and respect for the evidence of the text.

Postmodern approaches to *Measure for Measure* are most clearly seen in stage productions. There, you could think of it as simply 'a mixture of styles'. The label 'postmodern' is applied to productions that self-consciously show little regard for consistency in character, or for coherence in telling the story. Characters are often dressed in costumes from very different historical periods.

Postmodernism often revels in the cleverness of its own use of language, and accepts all kinds of anomalies and contradictions in a spirit of playfulness or 'carnival'. It abandons any notion of the organic unity of the play, and rejects the assumption that *Measure for Measure* possesses clear patterns or themes. Some postmodern critics even deny the possibility of finding meaning in language. They claim that words simply refer to other words, and so any interpretation is endlessly delayed (or 'deferred' as the deconstructionists say). Others focus on minor or marginal characters, or on loose ends, gaps or silences in the play, claiming that these features, often overlooked as unimportant, reveal significant truths about the play. Jonathan Dollimore, for example, notes that 'the prostitutes, the most exploited group in the society which the play represents, are absent from it'. And Kathleen McLuskie, discussing Jonathan Miller's production of *Measure for Measure* and his choice, as director, to have Isabella refuse the Duke's proposal and walk off the stage, makes a typically postmodern comment on theatre's 'constructed meaning':

> As a theatre director, he is aware of the extent to which the social meaning of a play depends upon the arrangements of theatrical meaning; which is different from simply asserting alternative 'interpretations'. The concept of interpretation suggests that the text presents a transparent view on to the real life of sexual relations whether of the sixteenth or the twentieth century. The notion of 'constructed meaning' on the other hand, foregrounds the theatrical devices by which an audience's perception of the action of the play is defined. The focus of critical attention, in other words, shifts from judging the action to analysing the process by which the action presents itself to be judged.

Organising your responses

The purpose of this section is to help you improve your writing about *Measure for Measure*. It offers practical guidance on two kinds of tasks: writing about an extract from the play and writing an essay. Whether you are answering an examination question, preparing coursework (term papers), or carrying out research into your own chosen topic, this section will help you organise and present your responses.

In all your writing, there are three vital things to remember. First, *Measure for Measure* is a play. Although it is usually referred to as a 'text', *Measure for Measure* is not a book, but a script intended to be acted on a stage. So your writing should demonstrate an awareness of the play in performance as theatre. Second, *Measure for Measure* is not a presentation of 'reality'. It is a dramatic construction in which the playwright, through theatre, engages the emotions and intellects of the audience. Through discussion of his handling of language, character and plot, your writing should reveal how Shakespeare uses themes and ideas, attitudes and values, to give insight into crucial social, moral and political dilemmas of his time – and yours.

The third thing to remember relates to how Shakespeare learned his craft. As a schoolboy, and in his early years as a dramatist, Shakespeare used all kinds of models or frameworks to guide his writing. But he quickly learned how to vary and adapt the models to his own dramatic purposes. This section offers frameworks that you can use to structure your writing. As you use them, follow Shakespeare's example! Adapt them to suit your own writing style and needs.

Writing about an extract

It is an expected part of all Shakespeare study that you should be able to write well about an extract (sometimes called a 'passage') from the play. An extract is usually between 30 and 70 lines long, and you are invited to comment on it. The instructions vary. Sometimes the task is very briefly expressed:

- Write a detailed commentary on the following passage.
  or
- Write about the effect of the extract on your own thoughts and feelings.

At other times a particular focus is specified for your writing:

- With close reference to the language and imagery of the passage, show in what ways it helps to establish important issues in the play.
  or
- Analyse the style and structure of the extract, showing what it contributes to your appreciation of the play's major concerns.

In writing your response, you must of course take account of the precise wording of the task, and ensure you concentrate on each particular point specified. But however the invitation to write about an extract is expressed, it requires you to comment in detail on the language. You should identify and evaluate how the language may offer hints to an actor concerning the building of personality, contributes to plot development, offers opportunities for dramatic effect, and embodies crucial concerns of the play.

The following framework is a guide to how you can write a detailed commentary on an extract. Writing a paragraph on each item will help you bring out the meaning and significance of the extract, and show how Shakespeare achieves his effects.

Paragraph 1: Locate the extract in the play and identify who is on stage.
Paragraph 2: State what the extract is about and identify its structure.
Paragraph 3: Identify the mood or atmosphere of the extract.
Paragraphs 4–8:
  Diction (vocabulary)
  Imagery
  Antithesis
  Repetition
  Lists

These paragraphs analyse how Shakespeare achieves his effects. They concentrate on the language of the extract, showing the dramatic effect of each item, and how the language expresses crucial concerns of the play.

Paragraph 9: Staging opportunities
Paragraph 10: Conclusion

The following example uses the framework to show how the paragraphs making up the essay might be written. The framework headings (in brackets in italics), would not of course appear in your essay. They are presented only to help you see how the framework is used. The extract is from Act 1 Scene 2, lines 106–74.

Extract

LUCIO Why, how now, Claudio? Whence comes this restraint?

CLAUDIO From too much liberty, my Lucio, liberty.
     As surfeit is the father of much fast,
     So every scope by the immoderate use
     Turns to restraint. Our natures do pursue   5
     Like rats that ravin down their proper bane
     A thirsty evil, and when we drink, we die.

LUCIO If I could speak so wisely under an arrest, I would send for
     certain of my creditors; and yet, to say the truth, I had as lief have
     the foppery of freedom as the morality of imprisonment. What's   10
     thy offence, Claudio?

CLAUDIO What but to speak of would offend again.

LUCIO What, is't murder?

CLAUDIO No.

LUCIO Lechery?   15

CLAUDIO Call it so.

PROVOST Away, sir, you must go.

CLAUDIO One word, good friend: Lucio, a word with you.

LUCIO A hundred, if they'll do you any good. Is lechery so looked
     after?   20

CLAUDIO Thus stands it with me. Upon a true contract
     I got possession of Julietta's bed –
     You know the lady, she is fast my wife,
     Save that we do the denunciation lack
     Of outward order. This we came not to   25
     Only for propagation of a dower
     Remaining in the coffer of her friends,
     From whom we thought it meet to hide our love
     Till time had made them for us. But it chances
     The stealth of our most mutual entertainment   30
     With character too gross is writ on Juliet.

LUCIO With child, perhaps?

CLAUDIO   Unhappily, even so.
    And the new deputy now for the Duke –
    Whether it be the fault and glimpse of newness,
    Or whether that the body public be   35
    A horse whereon the governor doth ride,
    Who, newly in the seat, that it may know
    He can command, lets it straight feel the spur;
    Whether the tyranny be in his place,
    Or in his eminence that fills it up,   40
    I stagger in – but this new governor
    Awakes me all the enrollèd penalties
    Which have, like unscoured armour, hung by th'wall
    So long that nineteen zodiacs have gone round
    And none of them been worn; and for a name   45
    Now puts the drowsy and neglected Act
    Freshly on me: 'tis surely for a name.
LUCIO   I warrant it is; and thy head stands so tickle on thy shoulders
    that a milkmaid, if she be in love, may sigh it off. Send after the
    Duke and appeal to him.   50
CLAUDIO   I have done so, but he's not to be found.
    I prithee, Lucio, do me this kind service:
    This day my sister should the cloister enter
    And there receive her approbation.
    Acquaint her with the danger of my state,   55
    Implore her, in my voice, that she make friends
    To the strict deputy: bid herself assay him.
    I have great hope in that; for in her youth
    There is a prone and speechless dialect
    Such as move men; beside, she hath prosperous art   60
    When she will play with reason and discourse,
    And well she can persuade.
LUCIO   I pray she may, as well for the encouragement of the like,
    which else would stand under grievous imposition, as for the
    enjoying of thy life, who I would be sorry should be thus foolishly 65
    lost at a game of tick-tack. I'll to her.
CLAUDIO   I thank you, good friend Lucio.
LUCIO   Within two hours.
CLAUDIO   Come, officer, away.

Paragraph 1: Locate the extract in the play and identify who is on stage.
This extract occurs immediately after the bawdy conversation between Lucio and the Gentlemen. Mistress Overdone has already revealed that Claudio has been arrested for 'getting Madam Julietta with child'. Shakespeare has reinforced that information by having Pompey repeat it with the news that all the brothels are to be 'plucked down'. To ensure that the audience is able to identify who is on stage, Pompey announces the arrival of Claudio, the Provost and Juliet.

Paragraph 2: State what the extract is about and identify its structure.
(Begin with one or two sentences identifying what the extract is about, followed by several sentences briefly identifying its structure, that is the different sections of the extract.)
    This extract concerns Claudio, the first person to be arrested under Angelo's strict new regime against fornication. Claudio and Juliet are being paraded publicly on Angelo's orders. Claudio explains his situation to his friend Lucio and speaks of the cause of his 'restraint' as being self-inflicted. Claudio then speculates upon Angelo's reasons for making an example of him. Claudio asks Lucio to persuade his sister to appeal for clemency to Angelo. He hopes that his sister's youth and eloquence will influence Angelo. Claudio's description of his plight is poetic; Lucio's replies are in prose and are typically cynical and reductive.

Paragraph 3: Identify the mood or atmosphere of the extract.
The mood of this extract changes as Claudio explains his 'crime' to his friend. His words are serious and thoughtful while Lucio's replies add a comic perspective to the episode. The fact that it is a public scene, with the silent Juliet as the other victim, adds dramatic tension. The single authoritative line spoken by the Provost reinforces the powerlessness of Claudio and Juliet.

Paragraph 4: Diction (vocabulary)
There is a marked contrast between the language and style of Claudio's words and those of Lucio. Claudio uses elaborate imagery and poetic form to express his complex thoughts and feelings, and there is a conflict between his awareness of his lack of restraint, and his commitment to Juliet. Lucio expresses his thoughts in prose, reflecting his more superficial attitude to Claudio's offence. For

example, he reduces Claudio's 'most mutual entertainment' to a 'game of tick-tack'. Lucio trivialises Claudio's imminent execution by saying it is as likely to happen as a milkmaid losing her virginity. Claudio uses language that avoids the suggestion that he had intended to commit the sin of fornication, speaking of Juliet as 'fast my wife', and he puns on the words 'restraint' and 'liberty', demonstrating a rueful acknowledgement of his faults. When speaking of Isabella's powers of persuasion, Claudio's choice of words is ironically ambiguous. He describes her youthfulness as convincing in itself. The word 'prone' has connotations of lying down receptively, in a way that can 'move' or arouse men.

Paragraph 5: Imagery

Claudio's speeches are full of unusual imagery. For example, he speaks of sexual desire as being like the effects of arsenical poison on rats, inducing greed for more: 'Like rats that ravin down their proper bane / A thirsty evil, and when we drink, we die'. He also probably intends a pun on 'die', which could mean orgasm. He describes the secrecy of the sin that he has been arrested for as the 'stealth of our most mutual entertainment', which now with 'character too gross is writ on Juliet', as though her pregnancy is written evidence of their intercourse. Speaking of Angelo's enforcement of old laws, Claudio compares the state to a 'horse whereon the governor doth ride', with Angelo as a rider asserting his mastery. In another image in the same speech he compares the old law to 'unscoured [unpolished, rusty] armour' in a time of peace, and then he personifies it: 'the drowsy and neglected Act'. Claudio's serious and complex imagery is undermined by Lucio's bawdy image of a milkmaid's 'head' (maidenhead).

Paragraph 6: Antithesis

The opening of this extract embodies one of the major oppositions of the play, that between 'liberty' and 'restraint'. These words are rich in connotations and Shakespeare plays with the various meanings implicit in the words. 'Restraint' for Lucio means the arrest of Claudio, but Claudio opposes it with the word 'liberty', meaning an excess of sexual licence. Claudio plays with variations on this antithesis and opposes 'surfeit' with 'fast' and 'scope' with 'restraint'. Lucio mockingly says he would prefer the 'foppery of freedom' to the 'morality of imprisonment'.

Paragraph 7: Repetition

'Liberty' and 'restraint' are two words that are repeated in this extract, emphasising that this antithesis embodies the central debate of the play. By repeating 'new' and 'newness', Claudio stresses the suddenness of Angelo's enforcement of the old laws against fornication. Claudio also repeats the word 'name', or reputation. Angelo's reputation for severity and austerity becomes a major motif of the play.

Paragraph 8: Lists

Shakespeare ensures that the audience is aware of the various possible motives for Angelo's tyranny. Claudio speculates on the alternative reasons for Angelo's enforcing of the laws against fornication in a list that becomes increasingly bitter as he considers the topic, concluding that Angelo has chosen to be severe only to enhance his own reputation. Claudio shows the urgency of his plight as he gives the list of instructions for Lucio: 'Acquaint her . . . / Implore her . . . / . . . bid herself assay him.'

Paragraph 9: Staging opportunities

There are several people on stage, with the central figures being Lucio and Claudio. There is also the Provost. In some productions, the Provost has Claudio handcuffed or tied to him. There are also guards and Juliet present. Observing them, perhaps from a safe distance, are Mistress Overdone and Pompey. This onstage audience offers opportunities for a director to make the conversation between Claudio and Lucio seem paradoxically private: by making it clear that they cannot hear the details of the discussion, or alternatively to suggest how much of his privacy Claudio has already lost by making him admit to everyone the nature of his relationship with Juliet. Juliet's vulnerability and shame are made more evident by her lack of speech.

Paragraph 10: Conclusion

This extract shows the effects of the Duke's abdication of power and Angelo's extreme severity. Claudio's arrest for getting pregnant a lady whom he seriously considers 'fast my wife' is explicitly contrasted with the preceding episode of bawdy conversation between the licentious soldiers and Lucio. This is Claudio's first appearance in the play and Shakespeare presents him as a serious and thoughtful young man who is well aware of his lack of 'restraint'. He is contrasted with Lucio, who has already been shown to be promiscuous. In this episode, though he is willing to do what he can to help Claudio, he appears unable to take even this situation seriously or to restrain himself from joking about it. Claudio's reasons for choosing Isabella to plead on his behalf become intensely and ironically significant in the subsequent episodes of the play.

Reminders

- The framework is only a guide. It helps you to structure your writing. Use the framework for practice on other extracts. Adapt it as you feel appropriate. Make it your own.
- Structure your response in paragraphs. Each paragraph makes a particular point and helps build up your argument.
- Focus tightly on the language, especially vocabulary, imagery, antithesis, lists, repetition.
- Remember that *Measure for Measure* is a play, a drama intended for performance. The purpose of writing about an extract is to identify how Shakespeare creates dramatic effect. What techniques does he use?
- Try to imagine the action. Visualise the scene in your mind's eye. But remember there can be many valid ways of performing a scene. Offer alternatives. Justify your own preferences by reference to the language.
- Who is on stage? Imagine their interaction. How do 'silent characters' react to what's said?
- Look for the theatrical qualities of the extract. What guides for actors' movements and expressions are given in the language? Comment on any stage directions.
- How might the audience respond? In Elizabethan times? Today? How might you respond as a member of the audience?
- How might the lines be spoken? Think about tone, emphasis, pace, pauses. Identify shifting moods and registers. Is the verse pattern smooth or broken, flowing or full of hesitations and abrupt turns?
- What is the importance of the extract in the play as a whole? Justify its thematic significance.

Writing an essay

As part of your study of *Measure for Measure* you will be asked to write essays, either under examination conditions or for coursework (term papers). Examinations mean that you are under pressure of time, usually having around one hour to prepare and write each essay. Coursework means that you have much longer to think about and produce your essay. But whatever the type of essay, each will require you to develop an argument about a particular aspect of *Measure for Measure*.

The people who read your essays (examiners, teachers, lecturers) will have certain expectations of your writing. They will know the play – you do not need to tell the story. In each essay they will expect you to discuss and analyse a particular topic, using evidence from the play to develop an argument in an organised, coherent and persuasive way. Examiners look for, and reward, what they call 'an informed personal response'. This simply means that you show you have good knowledge of the play ('informed') and can use evidence from it to support and justify your own viewpoint ('personal').

You can write about *Measure for Measure* from different points of view. As pages 84–106 show, you can approach the play from a number of critical perspectives (feminist, political, psychoanalytic, etc.). You can also set the play in its social, literary, political and other contexts, as shown in the Critical approaches section. You should write at different levels, moving beyond description to analysis and evaluation. Simply telling the story or describing characters is not as effective as analysing how events or characters embody wider concerns of the play. In *Measure for Measure*, these 'wider concerns' (themes, issues, preoccupations – or, more simply, 'what the play is about') include justice, mercy, and the potential threat to social order of unrestrained sexuality.

How should you answer an examination question or write a coursework essay? The following three-fold structure can help you organise your response:

opening paragraph
developing paragraphs
concluding paragraph.

Opening paragraph Begin with a paragraph identifying just what topic or issue you will focus on. Show that you have understood what the question is about. You probably will have prepared for particular topics. But look closely at the question and identify key words to see what particular aspect it asks you to write about. Adapt your material to answer that question. Examiners do not reward an essay, however well-written, if it is not on the question set.

Developing paragraphs This is the main body of your essay. In it, you develop your argument, point by point, paragraph by paragraph. Use evidence from the play that illuminates the topic or issue, and answers the question set. Each paragraph makes a point of dramatic or thematic significance. Some paragraphs could make points concerned with context or particular critical approaches. The effect of your argument builds up as each paragraph adds to the persuasive quality of your essay. Use brief quotations that support your argument, and show clearly just why they are relevant. Ensure that your essay demonstrates that you are aware that *Measure for Measure* is a play: a drama intended for performance, and therefore open to a wide variety of interpretations and audience response.

Concluding paragraph Your final paragraph pulls together your main conclusions. It does not simply repeat what you have written earlier, but summarises concisely how your essay has successfully answered the question.

Example

Question: '*Measure for Measure* changes nature half way through.' How far do you agree with Tillyard's view that only the first half of the play is successful?

The following notes show the 'ingredients' of an answer. In an examination it is usually helpful to prepare similar notes from which you write your essay, paragraph by paragraph. To help you understand how contextual matters or points from different critical approaches might be included, the words 'Context' or 'Criticism' appear before some items. Remember that Examiners are not impressed by 'name-dropping': use of critics' names. What they want you to show is your knowledge and judgement of the play and its contexts, and of how it has been interpreted from different critical perspectives. This question asks for your opinion, so there is no 'right' answer, but you must justify your response.

Opening paragraph

Show that you understand where and how the structure of *Measure for Measure* changes. You could argue that the first part of the play has all the elements of a tragedy, while the second half more clearly hints at resolution, and that the play could be classified as a tragicomedy. The question asks 'How far do you agree . . .?', so you will need to justify your interpretation of the ending of the play: for example, do you think that it ends with the 'successful' restoration of order and harmony? Do you think that the play suffers from the change in style?

Developing paragraphs

Now you should write a number of paragraphs on the structure of the play. In each paragraph you should identify how you would define the 'successful' nature of the first half the play, or comment on what you perceive to be the differences in style and nature of the second half. Some of the points that you could include are given below.

- Criticism Identify where and how critics suggest that the play changes in style and nature (Act 3 Scene 1, line 152 – see pages 90 and 102).
- Identify the style of the first half of the play, giving examples of what you consider to be the most important features.
- Context and political criticism Show how matters of current debate about justice, mercy and the proper governance of the self and state influence the workings of the plot. (See pages 89–90.)
- Criticism Discuss the way that the dramatic focus moves from Angelo and Isabella to the Duke, and the effects that this has on the play's language and imagery: particularly the contrast between the intensity of the debates between Angelo and Isabella and the later focus on the Duke's attempts to organise the other characters. Does the intensity return in Act 5?

- Comment on the effect of the introduction of new characters – Mariana and Barnardine – where new information has to be given to the audience.
- Performance criticism Show how the interpretation of the character of the Duke, Angelo or Isabella can influence the ending of the play. Have you seen contrasting performances? Give brief examples. (See pages 100–4.)
- Context Illustrate your understanding of the effect on the resolution of the play of Shakespeare's possible references to King James and the role of the ruler.

Concluding paragraph
Write several sentences pulling together your conclusions. Whether you feel that the change in the poetic style of the play makes only the first half successful might depend on your interpretation of Shakespeare's intentions, so you should ensure that you have made clear your thoughts about this. Whatever else your conclusion contains, you must describe the extent to which you agree or disagree with the question.

Writing about character

As the Critical approaches section showed, much critical writing about *Measure for Measure* traditionally focused on characters, writing about them as if they were living human beings. Today it is not sufficient just to describe their personalities. When you write about characters you will also be expected to show that they are dramatic constructs, part of Shakespeare's stagecraft. They help suggest the wider concerns of the play, have certain dramatic functions, and are set in a social and political world with particular values and beliefs. They reflect and express issues of significance to Shakespeare's society – and today's.

All that may seem difficult and abstract. But don't feel overwhelmed. Everything you read in this book is written with those principles in mind, and can be a model for your own writing. Of course you should say what a character seems like to you, but you should also write about how Shakespeare makes him or her part of his overall dramatic design. In *Measure for Measure*, one character or situation is frequently weighed or measured against another. For example:

- Angelo and Isabella are each forced unwillingly from a contemplative to an active role.
- The Duke and Angelo each thinks that he is above falling in love.
- Angelo and Isabella abhor fornication.
- Mariana takes Isabella's place in Angelo's 'garden-house'.
- Mariana's betrothal to Angelo reflects Juliet's to Claudio.
- Barnardine and Claudio are both condemned to die, each unwillingly.
- Ragozine's head is substituted for Claudio's.
- Angelo is twice given the task of substituting for the Duke.
- Angelo, Claudio and Lucio each marry the woman whose honour they have violated.

A different way of thinking of characters is that in Shakespeare's time, playwrights and audiences were less concerned with psychological realism than with character types and their functions. That is, they expected and recognised such stock figures of traditional drama as the ruler (the Duke), the maiden (Isabella) and the clown (Pompey). Today, film and television have accustomed audiences to expect the inner life of characters to be revealed. Although Shakespeare's characters do reveal thoughts and feelings, especially in soliloquy, his audiences tended to regard them as characters in a developing story, to be understood by how they formed part of that story, and by how far they conformed to certain well-known types and fulfilled certain traditional roles. In *Measure for Measure* there are few self-revelatory soliloquies, especially for the Duke.

It can be helpful to think of minor characters, whose roles are little more than functional. They are dramatic devices who briefly perform their part and then disappear from the play. For example, Friar Lawrence and Friar Peter help to establish the tone of religious commitment within the play. Though some critics draw attention to anti-monastic feeling in Jacobean times, it is not reflected in the play, where the Provost and Escalus show respect to friars. Mistress Overdone, Pompey and Froth represent the whole seedy underworld of vice in Vienna, though many directors include the non-speaking prostitutes who, for a modern audience, are the true victims of the corruption in Vienna. Barnardine's function is mainly comic, to balance the emotional suffering of Isabella who thinks that Claudio is dead, and allow us to see the merciful nature of the Duke.

Shakespeare shows that even a life like Barnardine's cannot be sacrificed to suit the Duke's convenience.

But there is also a danger in writing about the functions of characters or the character types they represent. To reduce a character to a mere plot device is just as inappropriate as treating him or her as a real person. In contrast with the minor characters, major characters have more extensive dramatic functions, and actors have far greater opportunities to create the stage illusion of a real person. When you write about characters in *Measure for Measure* you should try to achieve a balance between analysing their personality, identifying the dilemmas they face, and placing them in their social, critical and dramatic contexts. That style of writing is found all through this Guide, and that, together with the following brief discussions of four major characters, can help your own written responses to character.

The **Duke**'s character is concealed by the roles that he plays. In his first scene on stage he appears to be retiring from his duties with a haste that his deputies find shocking. His role in the first half of the play is a challenge to the actor playing the role as there is less personal information about the Duke, and more contradiction in his character, than for other major roles in Shakespeare's plays, though the Duke is the fifth longest part in all of his plays. For example, in the brief formal scene where the Duke is temporarily abdicating his power and place to Angelo, little is revealed about his character and he leaves any questions about his motives unanswered. He says only that he is leaving 'unquestioned / Matters of needful value' and that he has a strong dislike of crowds; he does not 'like to stage me to their eyes'. These two facts suggest someone who would avoid public occasions, yet the Duke does not abandon Vienna, but when disguised takes great interest in the conduct of his people. He also arranges a very public welcome for himself in Act 5.

In Act 1 Scene 3, the Duke gives Friar Thomas two possible reasons for his abdication of power, though he does say that there are others that he will reveal when he has more 'leisure'. One reason he gives is not very flattering to himself, as he speaks of his consciousness of the neglect of his public duties. He suggests that he is giving Angelo power to save his own reputation, and that his lax rule has led to anarchy:

And Liberty plucks Justice by the nose,
The baby beats the nurse, and quite athwart
Goes all decorum.   *(lines 30–2)*

But in the script there is little evidence of anarchy in Vienna.
Pompey's evasion of punishment is presented as comic rather than
completely evil. Mistress Overdone does not seem to be a particularly
successful bawd and her care for the child of Kate Keepdown is
charitable. The Duke's other reason for putting Angelo in charge of
Vienna is apparently to test his virtue: 'Hence shall we see, / If power
change purpose, what our seemers be' (Act 1 Scene 3, lines 54–5).

Lucio's description of the Duke as 'the old fantastical Duke of dark
corners' (Act 4 Scene 3, lines 147–8) can seem apt from an actor's
point of view as he searches for a convincing portrayal of him. There
are no revealing soliloquies in which the Duke communicates to the
audience his motives or feelings. In Acts 3 and 4, the Duke seems to
be responding to the situations he finds, rather than initiating action,
and his failure to convince Barnardine that he must be executed can
make him seem either ineffectual and foolish, or merciful, depending
on the playing of the part. His apparent cruelty in withholding from
Isabella the fact that Claudio is still alive adds another difficult
dimension to the interpretation of the Duke, as does his astonishing
proposal of marriage to her. However, Act 5 shows the Duke
completely in control of the action, and he publicly re-establishes his
authority on Vienna and on the play.

Angelo is reluctant at first to assume the supremely important role
given to him by the Duke: 'Let there be some more test made of my
metal / Before so noble and so great a figure / Be stamped upon it'
(Act 1 Scene 1, lines 48–50). However, after Scene 1 the audience is
shown the quick and brutal effects of his rule before he is himself
again on stage. His general reputation is of a man whose passions are
firmly under control, and the Duke describes him as 'a man of
stricture and firm abstinence' who 'scarce confesses / That his blood
flows, or that his appetite / Is more to bread than stone'. Lucio goes
much further, commenting cynically that his 'blood / Is very snow-
broth' and that 'when he makes water, his urine is congealed ice'.
Escalus feels that Angelo is so severe that he personifies 'Justice'. He
claims in soliloquy that he was proud of his reputation and his
'gravity' and that he has never been in love: 'Ever till now / When men

were fond, I smiled, and wondered how.' It is perhaps this refusal, or inability, to acknowledge his capacity for emotion that the Duke is testing. He claims to love Isabella, but his subsequent language is that of a rapist. He demands that Isabella submits to him, 'yielding up [her] body to [his] will', threatening to not only execute Claudio, but to torture him too, if she does not.

Angelo's first action on taking office seems to be the enforcement of old laws against fornication. Shakespeare suggests that he does this initially with draconian effect, destroying brothels and condemning Claudio to death. His inflexible personality makes him unable to see when mercy would be more appropriate, and also unable to resist his lustful feelings towards Isabella. It could be said that his earlier offence to Mariana is almost as unforgivable; in a time when marriage was the only option for a gently bred woman, not only does he abandon her, but he also claims that her reputation is questionable. The playing of Angelo presents a challenge to an actor because for much of the play his actions are unsympathetic. However, his soliloquies reveal to the audience his inner turmoil and sense of guilt about his failure to live up to his own standards, and have led some commentators to analyse his psychology as though he were a real person. His reactions at the end of the play are open to interpretation as his final words repeat his desire for death, and Shakespeare gives no suggestions about how he should respond to the Duke's injunction to 'Love' Mariana.

Isabella is another enigmatic character and she is measured against Angelo in her desire for restraint and choice of a sequestered life. Like Angelo, she reveals hidden passions. She demonstrates the accuracy of Claudio's description of her, in relation to both Angelo and the Duke:

> for in her youth
> There is a prone and speechless dialect
> Such as move men; beside, she hath prosperous art
> When she will play with reason and discourse,
> And well she can persuade. *(Act 1 Scene 2, lines 163–7)*

There are many puzzling questions about her character. Why does Shakespeare choose to make her a nun, unlike the young women in his source material? What is her motive for choosing a convent instead of the much more conventional choice of marriage, and asking for 'a more strict restraint'? Is her loathing for the 'vice' of fornication a rejection of her own sensuality, as hinted at in Act 2 Scene 4?

> were I under the terms of death,
> Th'impression of keen whips I'd wear as rubies,
> And strip myself to death as to a bed
> That longing have been sick for, ere I'd yield
> My body up to shame. *(lines 100–4)*

The questions about Isabella continue. Does her hysterical refusal to sacrifice herself for Claudio's life make her an unsympathetic character ('More than our brother is our chastity', Act 2 Scene 4, line 186)? Why does she agree to let Mariana risk her soul when she will not risk her own? What makes her decide to kneel by Mariana and plead for Angelo? How does she react when she first sees that Claudio is alive? Crucially, how does she respond to the Duke when he proposes marriage in Act 5? The script gives few clues to the actor, who must interpret the evidence about Isabella from her language, imagery and actions and other characters' reactions to her.

Lucio is another of the hotly debated characters of *Measure for Measure*. His name means 'light', and some modern theatre practitioners, such as Michael Bogdanov, have claimed that he brings illumination to the hypocrisy of the ruling classes, especially the Duke. The majority of critics, however, consider his function within the play is to add comic confusion, and also to show that the justice meted out by the Duke deals with those who are unrepentant. Lucio is apparently a loyal friend of Claudio's; he does what Claudio asks of him, and without his prompting Isabella would have abandoned Claudio to Angelo's justice. However, he refuses help to Pompey, presumably betrays Mistress Overdone, and abandons Kate Keepdown. He is witty and his language would suggest that he is an educated man not, like Pompey, 'a poor fellow that would live'. Lucio is unregenerate, and shows no awareness that he should feel guilt for his actions as a frequenter of brothels and betrayer of Kate Keepdown.

Characters embody social, political and moral issues of significance to Shakespeare's society – and today's. Isabella, Juliet, Mistress Overdone and Kate Keepdown are fictional characters in a drama, but, as feminist criticism shows, they represent attitudes to gender in Jacobean society. You should show your understanding of this and of the way that modern critics relate the play to current attitudes to gender. You should argue for your own view as to whether the Duke is devious or wise, cruel or merciful, an image of God or a machiavellian politician (and show you are aware of interpretations different from your own). But your writing should also show that the Duke represents particular attitudes to the role of a ruler in Jacobean society, for example King James strongly held the belief that absolute authority was his by divine right, but that concept of the ruler was equally strongly contested.

As always, never forget that *Measure for Measure* is a play. Even though characters embody particular themes, Shakespeare's language and imagery gives actors many opportunities to play characters in all kinds of different ways.

Resources

Books

Nigel Alexander, *Shakespeare: Measure for Measure*, Studies in English Literature Series, Edward Arnold, 1974
Gives a detailed discussion of the historical and social context of the play.

Cecily Berry, *The Actor and the Text*, Virgin, 1987
References to speaking the verse of *Measure for Measure* are scattered throughout. Useful for anyone studying Shakespeare, especially with a view to production. Berry's *Text in Action*, Virgin, 2001, contains even more practical approaches to analysing Shakespeare's language with an emphasis on speaking the words.

Kate Chedgzoy, *Measure for Measure*, Writers and Their Work Series, Northcote House, 2000
A particularly interesting discussion of the context of the play.

Kate Chedgzoy (ed.), *Shakespeare, Feminism and Gender*, New Casebook Series, Palgrave, 2001
Contains a brief but useful discussion of *Measure for Measure*.

Juliet Dusinberre, *Shakespeare and the Nature of Women*, 2nd edition, Macmillan, 1996
A feminist approach to the plays of Shakespeare and his contemporaries.

Terry Eagleton, *William Shakespeare*, Basil Blackwell, 1986
A demanding example of modern criticism that contains a brief discussion of *Measure for Measure* from the standpoint of the law and sexual politics.

Paul Edmundson, 'Comical and tragical', in S Wells and L C Orlin (eds.), *Shakespeare: An Oxford Guide*, Oxford University Press, 2003
Argues strongly against the genre of 'problem plays', and provides a valuable reading of *Measure for Measure*.

Darryl J Gless, *Measure for Measure, the Law and the Convent*, Princeton University Press, 1979
Explores the Christian context of *Measure for Measure*.

Andrew Gurr, *Studying Shakespeare: An Introduction*, Edward Arnold, 1988
A helpful approach to studying Shakespeare which concentrates on three plays, including *Measure for Measure*.

Russell Jackson and **Robert Smallwood** (eds.), *Players of Shakespeare 2*, Cambridge University Press, 1988
Includes Daniel Massey's account of playing the Duke in a Royal Shakespeare Company production of *Measure for Measure*.

Russell Jackson and **Robert Smallwood** (eds.), *Players of Shakespeare 3*, Cambridge University Press, 1993
Includes Roger Allam's account of playing the Duke in a Royal Shakespeare Company production of *Measure for Measure*.

Lisa Jardine, *Still Harping on Daughters*, Harvester Wheatsheaf, 1983
A historical and feminist approach to the plays of Shakespeare and his contemporaries.

Frank Kermode, *Shakespeare's Language*, Allen Lane, Penguin, 2000
A detailed examination of how Shakespeare's language changed over the course of his playwriting career. Contains a relatively brief discussion of the language of *Measure for Measure*.

Philip C McGuire, *Speechless Dialect – Shakespeare's Open Silences*, University of California Press, 1985
An influential study of productions of several plays by Shakespeare with a chapter on *Measure for Measure*.

Charles Marowitz, *Recycling Shakespeare*, Macmillan, 1991
An interesting and idiosyncratic discussion of transforming and adapting Shakespeare for the stage, which contains a discussion of *Measure for Measure* and the law.

Rosalind Miles, *The Problem of Measure for Measure*, Vision, 1976
Provides a thorough and detailed discussion of the context and critical history of the play.

Elizabeth M Pope, 'The Renaissance Background of Measure for Measure', in K Muir and S Wells (eds.), *Shakespeare Survey*, Cambridge University Press, 1982
Examines the historical and religious context of the play.

Carol Rutter and **Faith Evans**, *Clamorous Voices – Shakespeare's Women Today*, The Women's Press, 1998
Provides a fascinating account of two actors' contrasting approaches to playing Isabella.

Ernest Schanzer, *The Problem Plays of Shakespeare*, Routledge & Kegan Paul, 1963
An influential discussion of *Measure for Measure* as a 'problem play'.

Debora Kuller Shuger, *Political Theologies in Shakespeare's England*, Palgrave, 2001
A re-evaluation of the political and religious context of the play.

Caroline Spurgeon, *Shakespeare's Imagery and What It Tells Us*, Cambridge University Press, 1966 (first published 1935)
Now considered old-fashioned criticism, but still a useful starting point for the study of Shakespeare's imagery.

C K Stead (ed.), *Measure for Measure*, Casebook Series, Macmillan, 1971
A selection of critical essays covering a spectrum of critical opinion, including the essay by L C Knights.

David Lloyd Stevenson, *The Achievement of Shakespeare's Measure for Measure*, Cornell University Press, 1966
Concentrates particularly on re-establishing the status of *Measure for Measure* as one of Shakespeare's most important plays.

E M W Tillyard, *Shakespeare's Problem Plays*, Penguin, 1950
Slightly old-fashioned, but remains an interesting discussion of the 'problem plays'.

Cedric Watts, *Measure for Measure*, Penguin Masterstudies Series, Penguin, 1986
Detailed discussion of the play and its contexts.

Films and audio books

Measure for Measure (UK, 1982) Director: Desmond Davies. Kate Nelligan (Isabella), Tim Piggott-Smith (Angelo), Kenneth Coley (Duke). Made for the BBC Shakespeare Series.

Measure for Measure (UK, 1994) Director: David Thacker. Juliet Aubrey (Isabella), Corin Redgrave (Angelo), Tom Wilkinson (Duke). A modern interpretation produced for Channel 4.

Three major audio-book versions of the play are also available, in the series by Naxos, Arkangel and HarperCollins.

Measure for Measure on the Web
If you type 'Measure for Measure and Shakespeare' into your search engine, it may find over 56,000 items. Because websites are of wildly varying quality, and rapidly disappear or are created, no recommendation can be safely made. But if you have time to browse, you may find much of interest.